tALL STORY

CANDY
GOURLAY

tALL
stORY

A YEARLING BOOK

All rights reserved. Published in the United States by Yearling, an imprint of Random House Children's Books, a division of Random House, Inc., New York. Originally published in hardcover in Great Britain by David Fickling Books, an imprint of Random House Children's Books, a division of the Random House Group Ltd., London, in 2010 and subsequently published in hardcover in the United States by David Fickling Books, an imprint of Random House Children's Books, New York, in 2011.

Yearling and the jumping horse design are registered trademarks of Random House, Inc.

Visit us on the Web! www.randomhouse.com/kids

Educators and librarians, for a variety of teaching tools,
visit us at www.randomhouse.com/teachers

The Library of Congress has cataloged the hardcover edition of this work as follows:
Gourlay, Candy.
Tall story / Candy Gourlay. — 1st American ed.
p. cm.
Summary: Sixteen-year-old Bernardo, who is eight feet tall and suffers from a condition called Gigantism, leaves the Philippines to live with his mother's family in London, much to the delight of his thirteen-year-old half sister, Andi, a passionate basketball player.
ISBN 978-0-385-75217-6 (trade) — ISBN 978-0-385-75218-3 (lib. bdg.) —
ISBN 978-0-375-89847-1 (ebook)
[1. Giants—Fiction. 2. Size—Fiction. 3. Basketball—Fiction. 4. Culture conflict—Fiction.
5. Brothers and sisters—Fiction. 6. London (Eng.)—Fiction. 7. England—Fiction.
8. Philippines—Fiction.] I. Title.
PZ7.G7386Tal 2011
[Fic]—dc22
2010011891

ISBN 978-0-385-75233-6 (pbk.)

Printed in the United States of America
10 9 8 7 6 5 4 3 2 1

First Yearling Edition 2012

Random House Children's Books supports the First Amendment
and celebrates the right to read.

To Richard

Prologue
Andi

Rush hour.

So many armpits, so little deodorant. The whole world is heading out to Heathrow to meet long-lost relatives. I am wedged between the tummies of the two fattest men in the world.

Rank.

Mum's practically vibrating. Like she's overdosed on coffee. Which she probably has.

Dad's got his arm around her like a lock. She's fidgeting so hard and the train's so crowded. 'It'll be ages yet, Mary Ann,' he whispers into her ear.

'I just want to make sure we're there when he comes out.'

'He's sixteen. He'll be fine!'

Dad kisses her forehead. Which isn't a stretch because the crowd is pushing them so close together his face is practically pasted to her head.

'But William' – Mum glares at his chin – 'he's so TALL!'

Why is Mum so psycho about Bernardo being tall? She's been going on about it since we found out he was coming to London. 'Don't be surprised now, Andi, your brother is tall. *Tall*, you hear me?'

Does she think I needed impressing? I mean, Mum isn't exactly God's gift to the human race in the height department. I'm the smallest in Year Eight and I'm still taller than her. She's so short she needs an ID to prove she's old enough to buy wine at the supermarket. 'I don't understand,' she always argues at the Tesco Express. 'Where I come from, there's never any problem.'

Well, London isn't the Philippines, Mum.

The two tummies are practically holding me up in the carriage. I could fall asleep and remain vertical. Hopefully it won't be this bad on the return trip with Bernardo and his luggage.

Bernardo!

I can't believe I'm minutes away from becoming someone's little sister.

If he's tall like Mum says, he's guaranteed to love Michael Jordan. She says everyone in the Philippines is mad about basketball and I'm Michael Jordan's biggest fan. And maybe with another teenager in the house, we can listen to normal music instead of selections from Mum and Dad's pre-Jurassic collection. And now there will be someone else to ignore the bad Dad-jokes that for some reason make Mum go hysterical.

I'm tired of being the Only Child.

And then suddenly the train is screeching to a stop at Heathrow and Mum's dragging me out from between the two tummies. It's miles to walk through all those long, long tunnels to Terminal 3. Then we have to wait an hour before Bernardo's plane number shows on the arrival boards. Then it's another half-hour before they say 'Baggage in Hall'. Now Mum's staring at luggage tags to see which people emerging from the gate were on the plane from the Philippines. 'Look, look!' she screams (and it's no use telling Mum she's loud: she was born with no volume control).

And then she stands there for ages holding the welcome banner up high, hopping a little on one leg like she really, really needs to go to the toilet.

Dad puts his arm around Mum's shoulders and whispers in her ear some more. But her eyes are glazed. She's beyond help.

And then she screams so sharply that people nearby stop kissing and hugging to stare.

'THERE HE IS! OH, NARDO! OH, NARDO! OH! OH! OH!'

And I squint past all the huggers and kissers in the Arrivals hall, through the tiny panes of glass on the double doors, and all I can see is some geek's necktie. But Mum's already dropped her banner and she's CRAWLING under the barrier and rushing towards the necktie, all the while squealing something in Tagalog. Dad's got the banner now; he's holding it up and grinning so broadly you can see that he's missing a canine.

Then I finally *get* why Mum goes on and on about Bernardo being tall.

Rocky, the captain of my basketball team, is TALL.

Michael Jordan is TALL.

But Bernardo is no way tall like Rocky or Michael Jordan.

Bernardo is a GIANT.

Part One

Be Careful What You Wish For

1
Bernardo

I have a mother. And a younger sister. And a step-father named William.

But they live in London, on the other side of the world. And I live here, with my uncle and aunt, in the village of San Andres, a barrio so small it is barely a mosquito bite on the mountains of Montalban in the Philippines.

For years I've been waiting for the day when the British Home Office will see fit to write me the letter saying, *Yes please, Bernardo, come to London and be with your family.* But it's been years and years and I'm six-teen now anyway and the letter has not come, and sometimes I think it will never come, which is just as well because the way things are, leaving San Andres is not an easy thing.

We are a village usually noticed not for what we have but for what we don't: we have no square, no supermarket, no bar, no church – the nearest confessional being over the next hill in the barrio of

San Isidro. The houses don't have much either: no clay-tiled roofs, not much paint left on the old planked walls, no tidy pavements outside each rusty garden gate.

Bernardo was my dead father's name, the only thing that once belonged to him that I claim as my own. This I explain to anyone who will listen. But nobody ever does.

Your name is Bernardo? God be praised! Bernardo Carpio!

Bernardo Carpio? No, no! I say. *My name is Bernardo, after my father. And my surname is not Carpio. It's Hipolito. Hi-po-li-to.* Bernardo Carpio is a giant, everyone knows that. He's a story, an old legend.

And then they laugh. They laugh because they look at me: they look at my feet so wide and so long I can only wear sandals made specially by Timbuktu the tailor, they look at my shoulders, rounded from the effort of squeezing through low doors, they look up, up, up to the top of my huge head . . . and they know better.

I'll bet Bernardo Carpio, the giant, never used to be the smallest in his class.

The year that I was thirteen, it seemed as if all the other boys in my class had taken a dose of Super-Gro, the miracle plant food used by farmers to fatten up their crops. Everyone was suddenly shooting up like weeds, arms and legs thickening like tree trunks. Jabby too.

In fact, Jabby was a whole head and shoulders taller than me and he liked slinging an arm over my shoulders to prove the point. He even had hair under his armpits and he carried a can of Rexona spray deodorant in his bag, like a hidden weapon. His voice dipped an octave. Suddenly he was tall enough to get into eighteen-rated movies and tall enough to talk to girls. The Mountain Men, which was the local basket-ball team, signed him up.

Meanwhile, I remained small and squeaky and hairless as a just-born pup.

'It's nothing to worry about, it's only a matter of time,' Auntie Sofia had said. 'We're not tall people. Look at your ma. She's tiny. Look at *me*.'

And I looked at Auntie's squat pumpkin figure and my anxiety increased a hundredfold.

So when I finally started growing, it was as if my body had been held back against its will and was making up for lost time.

Two inches in one month. Four inches in two months. And so on. At night when everything was silent, I could hear a soft noise. *Creak creak creak.* My bones were lengthening, pulling and stretching my muscles like dough from the bakery.

The year I turned fourteen, Mama came to visit for a few weeks.

I was six foot tall. Taller than Uncle Victor. Taller than Jabby. 'I told you it was only a matter of time,' Auntie said smugly.

We took Uncle's jeepney to the International Airport. Sitting on the rear bench used to be a peril, what with the potholes and the jeepney's nonexistent shock absorbers. Auntie bounced around in the front seat like a Ping-Pong ball in a jar. I kept from being shaken to pieces by wedging myself firmly in place with my long legs. Being tall had its advantages.

The International Airport building was fancy enough, though slums girdled it like a tattered skirt. We were herded into a fenced-off area with other meeters and greeters just opposite the smart Arrivals terminal. Security guards kept the crowds at bay.

The holding pen seethed with waving hands and lips blowing kisses and hard elbows and crumpled *Welcome Home!* banners.

I didn't have to fight my way to the front. That was another advantage of being tall. I could see clearly enough over the crowd.

'Is she there yet?' Auntie called up to me, cupping her mouth as if she was shouting up a mountain.

'Wait . . . let me see.'

And there she was.

She was so tiny her wheelie bag seemed almost double her size. Ma bundled a coat under one arm and gazed into the crowd, shielding her eyes from the sun.

'Ma! Ma!'

I waved my arms and her face brightened. She waved excitedly and began to drag her bag across to the holding pen, her eyes fixed on mine.

'Pardon.' I pushed a path through the crowd, with Auntie and Uncle following in my wake like a conga line. 'Excuse us.'

I straightened my back. Ma would be so proud when she got a good look at me. Two years ago on her last visit, I came up to her shoulders, I was that small. She was going to be so surprised. She was going to say, *Well done, Bernardo. You are on your way to becoming a man.*

As she drew nearer her eyes grew wider, but the

look on her face was not that of amazement. Instead, Ma bit her lip and stared at me like I had grown a third eye on my forehead. I bent down and put my arms around her and she stood on her toes and reached up to my shoulders. 'Oh, Nardo, you . . . you're so tall!'

'It must be his diet,' declared Auntie as she scurried around to embrace her sister. 'You know I've been giving him a glass of evaporated milk every morning since he was a baby!'

But later that evening after we'd opened all the presents and they thought I'd gone to bed, I heard them arguing.

'I think he should see a doctor, Sofia.'

'There's nothing wrong with him, Mary Ann. He's a happy, normal boy.'

'His father was barely five foot eight! How can he have grown to six?'

'His friends have grown taller too. You should see them.'

'But there's something wrong. He should see an endocrinologist!'

'Endo-what? Sister, you're full of medical mumbo jumbo.'

'Mumbo jumbo? I'm a nurse!'

Later that week, Ma took me to see a doctor in the city. He set about measuring me, from the circumference of my head to the size of my feet.

When he'd finished, he sat down and folded his hands over his stomach. 'There is nothing wrong with this boy,' he said, his nose twisted as if she had made a bad smell. 'The youth of today are bound to exceed their parents in height.'

'But he's only fourteen.' Suddenly Ma sounded uncertain. 'I'm a nurse, sir. I just think it's highly unusual—'

'A nurse? What sort of nurse?'

'I work in an emergency room.'

'Well, I can tell you there's no emergency here.' The doctor waved dismissively. 'You are too anxious. Relax.'

Ma pressed her lips together. Guilt prickled the back of my neck as she paid a hundred and fifty pesos to the secretary outside the doctor's office. She didn't say another word during the two-hour bus ride back to San Andres.

Before she got on the plane to London, Ma turned to Auntie. 'Sofia, if Nardo grows any taller, I want you to let me know.'

'He'll be fine, Mary Ann,' Auntie said. 'Don't worry

your pretty little head. We'll look after Bernardo. We always do. Now shoo! You'll be late for your flight.'

'Promise me!'

Auntie promised.

And I'm sure she really intended to keep that promise.

But then people began to make the connection between me and Bernardo Carpio.

'The spirit of Bernardo Carpio has returned in you, Nardo,' Old Tibo, the barber, told me. 'San Andres has always prayed for Bernardo Carpio to return, and now he has.'

And it was Tibo who pointed out the absence of earthquakes. 'Since the boy began to grow, the earthquakes have stopped. This boy has saved the barrio.'

And the people came.

And they brought gifts.

And they made me their hero.

And Auntie put off taking me to the doctor and I didn't tell Mum what was going on, and Auntie and Uncle didn't say anything either and we made sure we never sent photographs that made my height too obvious because what would Ma say if she knew that I was now eight foot?

2
Andi

Height isn't everything, Dad says. And don't I know it!

'I'm taking a risk, Andi,' Coach said. 'Seeing as you're the shortest and the youngest on the team.'

True. I was the shortest and the youngest.

But he still picked me.

I was *point guard*!

Point guard. Point guard. *POINT GUARD!*

Dream come true, hallelujah!

I was so excited I ran all the way home from the school courts, ignoring the usual London drizzle-that-wasn't. I ran up all the six flights of stairs to our flat. And I did a pirouette right there, on the landing outside our door. Had any of the neighbours peeked down the stairwell, they would have seen me, one toe of my Air Jordans pointing up and my basketball shorts swirling around my knees.

Point guard!

And me only in Year Eight!

HISTORIC!

The door opened. Mum was home from the night shift. I threw myself into her arms.

'You won't believe what just happened.'

Jinx! We said exactly the same thing at the same time! We both laughed so hard someone in the flat next door thumped on the wall to shut us up.

'What happened, Mum?' I said at last.

'You first,' she said.

'No, *you* first!'

There was a sharp whistling noise. The kettle was boiling in the kitchen.

'Wait . . . let me get that.' Mum hurried into the kitchen, which was also the hallway cupboard with all the coats and bags draped on a forest of hooks. What did that oily estate agent say? 'Compact but so spacious you would be surprised.' That was probably because HE was surprised. The flat was a shoebox.

Point guard!

All that hard work had finally paid off. All those training sessions. Showering in Coach's spit as he yelled at us. Breathing in the aroma of sweaty armpits, dirty rubber balls, unchanged socks and old trainers.

'Do you fancy some tea, Andi?' Mum called.

'Yes, thanks, Mum. Two sugars.'

Mum bustled around the dining-room table, taking out two mugs and clearing aside a pile of ironing and a postcard just arrived from the Philippines. The postcard had a photograph of a concrete dome surrounded by banana trees.

Amandolina, it said. *This is the new basketball arena that is being built in San Andres. Wish you were here. Your loving brother, Bernardo.*

Mum laid a steaming mug of tea in front of me and sat down.

'So what's so awesome, Mum? Is it about Bernardo?'

Highly unlikely, of course. Mum's been trying to get Bernardo cleared by the Home Office since I was born. It would take a massive miracle to sort *that* problem out.

'No, of course not. But it's still great news.' Mum's eyes shone.

'Oh?' I held my breath and crossed the fingers on both my hands. Dared I hope? Could it be . . .

'*We got the house!*'

'YES!' I leaped to my feet so suddenly that some of the ironing slipped onto the floor. Mum and I were too busy hopping up and down to care. 'Yes, yes, YES!'

'No more queuing for the loo!'

'No more eating with the ironing on the table!'

'Our own front door!'

'MY OWN ROOM!'

We collapsed, breathless, into our chairs.

The oily estate agent had taken us to see the house only last week. It was a *palace* compared to this dump!

I couldn't believe it when Mum and Dad said they'd put in an offer. The estate agent raised an eyebrow like he'd found a black spot on a banana. There were so many other interested buyers, he warned, we shouldn't get our hopes up.

'It all came together today.' Mum flicked a tear from her cheek. 'The estate agent called this morning. He said we could have the house at the lower price if we could move quickly.'

'That's awesome, Mum!'

'They wanted to exchange contracts by next week.'

'Great!'

'So we're moving in two weeks!'

Two weeks?

Suddenly it was as if all the air had pumped out of my lungs. I tried to take a deep breath but I couldn't.

'What do you mean, we're moving in two weeks?'

'There was another buyer, but in the end the house

owner went with us because we agreed to all the conditions . . .'

'What conditions?'

'Well, he wanted us to . . .' Mum launched into a list that made my eyes glaze over almost immediately. The words 'cash payment' and 'speedy' jumped out. I shook myself.

'But what about school? I can't leave in the middle of term, can I?'

'No worries! I made some phone calls. You start at Saint Simeon's the day after we move.'

My voice sounded far away, like it was coming from outside, on the landing. 'But what about the basketball team . . . ?'

'I know it's a bit sudden,' Mum beamed. 'But, Andi, the timing is perfect. The sooner we move, the better. Someday we'll need an extra bedroom for Bernardo. And you'll *love* Saint Simeon's.'

I sat very, very still.

'What was *your* good news, darling?' Mum said.

3
Bernardo

It was while we young boys sat waiting our turn on the long bench at the barbershop that Old Tibo told stories about Bernardo Carpio the giant.

To start with, everybody *hated* Bernardo Carpio, Old Tibo said. He would unfold his fingers and count off the reasons why the giant had been so reviled.

1. The people feared him because he was different.
2. He was a little bit magic. His mother was human, but his father? They weren't so sure. He was from elsewhere, foreign. They had no goodwill towards him, even after he died.
3. And of course Bernardo was a freak, a monster.

'How many times did the townspeople try to drive Bernardo Carpio out of San Andres?' Old Tibo would say, stabbing his razor in the air. 'They poisoned his well. They stoned his fruit so that it fell to the ground and rotted before it was ripe. They even stole his dog.'

Which was so appalling that all the boys on the waiting bench looked at each other in horror.

But Bernardo Carpio refused to be driven out.

His late mother was born in San Andres and so was he. To live in the village was his right.

'But what could he do? How could he win the people to his side?' Old Tibo would stop snipping and turn to his audience. 'Instead of fighting back with anger, he decided to fight back with kindness. He was going to make the villagers love him. He was going to become their hero.'

One morning the farmers of San Andres woke to find that their fields had been ploughed. In the night, Bernardo had run his comb through the soil and turned the earth into furrows.

A river ran on the other side of the hill but not close enough to irrigate the fields. Bernardo pushed his finger into the side of the mountain and carved a stream from the river down to the fields, bringing irrigation and fresh water to the village. 'If you look closely at the hillside,' Old Tibo said, 'you can just see giant footprints where he trod.'

The fields lay in the deep shadow of a valley, and as a result, the crops of San Andres grew stunted and pale from lack of sun. So Bernardo planted his huge hands on the two mountains that shaded the valley and pushed them apart, just enough to let in the sun. To this day, hand-shaped indentations remain on the mountain slopes.

'Bernardo was a blessing,' Old Tibo said. 'And he was right: not only did the villagers come to love him, they came to realize that they *needed* him.'

One terrible monsoon, when rain lashed the village like a vicious whip and many coconut trees lost their crowns in the storms, the Earth began to shake. A few quakes here and there at first. And then, every day, a great shuddering.

One day the village shook so violently that houses crumbled as if they were made of sugar. Across the main road, a huge crack appeared, steam hissing out in clouds. Peering down into the fissure, the villagers saw two moving walls of rock about to collide with each other, like a pair of monumental hands poised to clap. It would have been a collision so powerful as to destroy San Andres completely.

The earth began to shake again, and everyone closed their eyes tight, said their prayers and waited for the end.

But nothing happened.

When they opened their eyes they saw, deep down in the fissure, Bernardo Carpio, arms braced against the two walls of stone, his face twisted with determination.

And then the granite lip of the fissure crumbled, and rock and earth caved into the crack. And they never saw Bernardo again.

But the village was saved.

4
Andi

Coach came round to talk to Mum and Dad.
    I sat outside on the landing, listening hard,
but they never raised their voices loud enough for me
to hear, and when Coach reappeared he was all
smiles and Good Luck With Your Move and
Congratulations On Your New Home and shaking
hands, so I knew that he had totally lost the
battle before even beginning the war. Mum
and Dad stood in the doorway grinning their best
grins.

'And thanks for dropping by!' Mum said brightly as
Coach and Dad shook hands.

'Thanks, Coach,' I muttered as he went past.
Thanks for nothing.

He avoided my eyes and raised his shoulders.
'Sorry, Andi.' And then he edged past me and down
the stairs like a guilty man.

'Oh, Andi, Andi, *Andi*,' Mum said. 'Come and
have a hug.'

I hated it when she treated me like a toddler. But I went and had a hug anyway.

'Well done for getting point guard,' Dad said, ruffling my hair the way he would a dog's. 'But we can't pass up this chance to move. This flat is a cupboard, we have no choice. You know that.'

'I know.' I rubbed my eyes.

'Come on in,' Mum said. 'I'll get supper on the table.'

I followed them back into the flat. 'It's just . . . I've been working *hard* to get Coach to pick me. I've been *slaving* away . . .'

'I know, darling.' Dad began to lay the table for dinner.

Mum lit the stove and measured some rice into a pot, sighing. 'Ah well. It was inevitable really, wasn't it?'

I stiffened. 'What do you mean, *inevitable*?'

'Oh, you know, you're not exactly basketball-player material.'

I stared at her.

'Mum, I made point guard. It's not about height, it's about skill.'

'Mary Ann,' Dad said urgently, but Mum ignored him.

'I know, I know. Skill. But you've also got to be tall. Basketball players have to be TALL.'

'*Mary Ann!*' Dad groaned.

'What?' Mum looked up from the stove. 'I'm just saying.'

'MUM, they made me POINT GUARD!' I banged my fists on the table, making all the plates jangle.

'ANDI!'

Mum glared at me like *I* was the annoying one.

'Andi, sweetheart, we're so sorry you had to leave the team,' Dad said hurriedly. 'Mum's just—'

'I'm just telling the truth!' she whirled furiously at him.

Dad ignored her outburst. 'Mum's just *brainstorming.*'

'Yeah. Right.' I scowled at them. 'It's not about height, Mum. I'm *good* at basketball . . . which you would know if you ever came to see me play.'

Mum didn't reply, but she glowered at Dad like it was all *his* fault.

I walked out. Which is hard in a flat as small as ours. It was only one small step into the sitting room. At least there was a door, which I tried to slam, but it wouldn't even close properly because Dad's bedroom slippers were in the way. I kicked them into

26

the kitchen and the door thudded shut. As if on cue, Mum and Dad's voices rose in sharp argument.

They had no idea how important basketball was to me. Mum never came to any of my games. Dad came once or twice but neither of them was ever *around* enough to see if I was any good or totally rank. And now I had to give it up. Saint Simeon's website mentioned football, hockey, netball ... but not basketball.

The new house was just round the corner from the Northern Royal Hospital, where both Mum and Dad worked as casualty nurses. They were always working. Night shifts and twelve-hour shifts and this shift and that shift.

We weren't just moving so we could have more room. We were moving so they could do even MORE shifts.

I felt a twinge. I couldn't even resent that fact without a pinch of guilt. I mean, they were working all hours *saving lives*! I was like Lois Lane wanting a snog when Superman had to go off and save the world. It was so unfair. Why was it *me* who had to feel guilty all the time?

Well.

To be honest, I knew that I was the lucky one.

I was the one who got to live with them . . . instead of being on the other side of the world like poor Bernardo, waiting for ever and ever for the Home Office to let him come to England.

I mean, *sixteen years* he's been waiting!

I feel guilty about *that* too.

There were photos of Bernardo on the mantelpiece.

Bernardo as a baby with spiky black hair.

Bernardo on Mum's lap.

Bernardo with toddler me, that one year Mum took me to the Philippines.

And Bernardo at fourteen, all bad teeth, bad skin and big head, sitting in a restaurant with Mum.

He looked like any regular kid on a day out with his mother. Except of course he only got to see Mum every two years.

Which has always made me feel extra, *extra* guilty.

And next to the Bernardo pictures was a picture of the *other* Bernardo.

He was a solemn-looking man with a short haircut and Chinese eyes. Ever since I can remember, his picture has been on the mantelpiece. Which is kind of creepy, because of course Mum isn't married to *him* any more.

The other Bernardo belonged to Mum's other life, a long, long time ago in a galaxy far, far away. Well, in the Philippines anyway. He was Bernardo's dad.

Mum and Dad's wedding picture stood off to the right and a little to the back behind a ceramic vase.

Dad didn't seem to mind having the picture up there. He acted like it was the most natural thing in the world for his wife's ex-husband to take centre stage on the mantelpiece.

Yeugh.

Apparently soon after little Bernardo was born, both Mum and Bernardo Senior fell ill with dengue fever. That's one of the diseases you can get by being bitten by a mosquito, of which there are plenty in the Philippines, so Mum says.

Mum was so ill, her sister Sofia had to look after baby Bernardo while she was taken away to hospital.

She woke up many days later and her doctor told her, 'The good news is you are now immune to the dengue mosquito that infected you. The bad news is there are four strains of dengue fever. One down and three to go.'

Which would have been a hilarious thing to say had it not been for the fact that, unlike Mum, the husband named Bernardo had not woken up from the fever.

He was dead.

Mum said it was the worst time in her life.

She was ill, bereaved, with a tiny baby to look after.

And she was broke.

She had to borrow gazillions to pay the hospital bills. Nurses in the Philippines don't earn gazillions and she *owed* gazillions. It was dire.

One night she saw a comet flashing through the sky and she made a wish. She wished she could earn enough money to pay back the debt.

The very next day the job in England came up.

Her wish had come true.

She left baby Bernardo with Auntie, thinking that she could send for him when the time was right. But it never happened.

Then of course she married Dad and had me.

She's been trying to bring Bernardo over to England for as long as I remember. But it's been a mission. Years of paperwork and overseas phone calls (most of which seemed to consist of Mum going, 'Hello? Hello? Can you hear me now, Sofia?'). Mum will bore anyone willing to listen with the saga of getting Bernardo's immigration papers.

So though her wish came true, it took Bernardo away from her.

Maybe that's the way wishes work.

I wished for point guard.

Mum wished for a house.

We both got our wishes. But one good thing deleted the other, like a finger falling on the wrong computer key.

Oops.

5
Bernardo

It was almost midnight.

The chirping of crickets and the buzz of snoring from upstairs combined into the usual night chorus.

. I sat at the kitchen table, postcard and pen in hand, staring at Mum's photograph on the wall. It had been hanging there for so long the red of the London bus had been bleached to pink. I was racking my brains for something more intelligent to write than just *wish you were here*, even though that's all I ever wanted to write because it was true.

I wished she was here. And Uncle William. And Amandolina.

Actually, I wished *I* was *there* more than I wished *they* were *here*. When Ma sent photos from London, Auntie often sniffed and said London looked too grand, too cold, too hurried, too posh. But I didn't care. And it wasn't that San Andres was too rough, too hot, too slow or too tired either. Home is wherever Ma is, and home was where I wanted to be.

Tap tap.

Who was that tapping at the window? It was far too late, even for Jabby. But then Jabby was perfectly capable of sneaking out at night on some crazy impulse. I cast a sidewards glance at the window and started.

It was wide open; the mosquito screens that Auntie usually kept fastened gaped outwards into the black night.

'*Psst.* Giant Boy!' The whisper wafted in like a slight breeze.

The voice was unmistakable. Mad Nena! What was she up to? I bowed my head, fixing my eyes on the postcard as if I hadn't heard, hoping she would go away.

'Psst. I know you can hear me.'

The casement suddenly swung hard against a nearby table. Goose pimples pricked the back of my neck.

'So. Can you hear me now?'

I stood up.

In the shadows beyond the windowsill, Mad Nena's head was a dark lump; the peering eyes watched me greedily, the way they watched me every day from around street corners and behind trees, following my every move.

I hurried over, glancing up the stairs. Should I call for Uncle and Auntie? But then what would Mad Nena tell them? She stood in the yellow square of light cast by my window, her bony arms hugging herself tight.

I cleared my throat. 'Sister Nena . . . ma'am . . . my auntie will not . . .'

'You know as well as I do that she's gone to bed. *Hero*.'

I swallowed. My hands were suddenly cold, like I'd plunged them into a bucket of ice.

'Please don't call me that.'

'Hero? But that's what you are. Bernardo, who's going to save our town from calamity.'

'Please don't.'

'Do you feel guilty, Giant Boy? Guilty about Gabriela? Guilty for what you did to me?'

'Look, Sister, I'm sorry,' I mumbled. 'I'm sorry for everything.' I wished now that Auntie would suddenly appear. *Nena, what are you doing?* she would say. *Shoo! Shoo!*

I could easily have called for Auntie over my shoulder.

But I didn't.

It was after Gabriela died that Nena started

34

wandering the streets. She wore the same clothes until they melted into rags. At the oddest times, and for no obvious reason, she would yell and weep. Then she would begin to sing her strange, wordless songs. Her most treasured possession was a laminated card that someone had given her at Gabriela's funeral. She wore it around her neck on a red ribbon. It had Saint Gertrude's prayer on it, the one that released a thousand souls from Purgatory every time it was prayed.

Whenever I saw Nena on the street, I crossed to the other side. 'She's harmless, Nardo,' Auntie chided. 'She can't do anything to you now.'

But tonight the eyes gazing at me through the matted hair were clear.

'I'm sorry,' I said again, reaching to shut the casement. 'I think you should go.'

'I forgive you,' she whispered.

I stopped.

'S-sorry?'

'No hard feelings.'

'What . . . what do you want from me?'

Behind the tangle of hair, the eyes glowed like embers of coal.

'I want nothing from you. I bring you a gift, Hero. A gift.'

She reached up and pulled my hand from the sill, pushing something firmly into my palm.

It was the wishing stone.

For a moment I could see Gabriela again, dark eyes flashing, long hair black and silky as a stream . . . and the wishing stone, nestled in the cleft bared by her lavishly unbuttoned blouse.

It felt solid and heavy in my hand.

'No,' I whispered. 'I can't take this.'

'This is yours. Gabriela wanted me to give it to you. That much she told me before she died.'

It looked like any stone one would find on a beach. A stone for skipping in the sea. A stone for loading in a slingshot to dislodge ripe fruit from the tops of the mango trees. But I knew its power. I knew what it could do.

'It will grant you one wish. *One wish*. What is your heart's desire?'

Longing swelled in my chest so suddenly, I almost winced. My heart's desire? Wasn't it obvious? Everyone knew what I wanted more than anything else.

'I can't accept this . . .' I said faintly. But inside my head there was a clamour. *Take it! Take it!* . . .

'She wanted *you* to have it. It was her dying wish.'

'But . . .'

'It's yours, Hero.'

And then she quickly jumped down from her perch and ran to the yawning gate of our house.

'Nardo?'

I stared at her dazedly.

'Be careful what you wish for.'

She laughed a silent laugh, her shoulders shaking, her mouth open wide. She slapped her knee and waved, then stepped out into the muddy darkness.

6
Andi

'You'll love it at Saint Sim's,' Dad said. 'They've got a new gym.'

We were driving across town in our Toyota, which would have been another good surprise for our oily estate agent because it was a teacup on wheels.

Lucky Dad. The most comfortable seat was the driver's: Mum didn't want to drive and of course I couldn't.

Mum sat under a large wheelie bag in the front passenger seat. And I was in the back, buried under an avalanche of duvets. Which was probably the safest thing in case of an accident, as long as I didn't suffocate first.

The moving lorry was to follow later in the afternoon. It was ten times the size of our flat but we didn't have any trouble filling it up.

'Yes!' Mum said. 'They offer so many sports! You can easily pick one where height is not an advantage. Table tennis. Bowling. Ukulele.'

'Ukulele is not a sport, Mum!'

'But it's small – it's perfect for you.'

'MUM!'

Maybe she was trying to be funny.

'Here we are!' Dad said.

We pulled over but it took ages for Mum to liberate herself from the suitcase and me from the bedding. Dad tried to help but ended up getting Mum's heel on his big toe. When we were finally free, we all turned to stare at our new home.

It was even bigger than I remembered. Three floors of living space. Three bedrooms. With steps leading up to a front door which was double the width of our flat. The windows were so clean they winked in the sun.

Dad was like a little boy with a new toy. He grabbed Mum's hand and pulled her up to the front steps. She shrieked as he swung her easily into his arms like a doll.

'Dad!' I blushed. They were so rank. Worse than teenagers. I glanced around surreptitiously to see if any of the neighbours' curtains were twitching.

'Can't a man carry his bride over the threshold of their new home?' He beamed at Mum.

'Oh, William,' she giggled like an idiot.

I folded my arms across my chest and waited for them to stagger through the door or for Dad's back to cave in, whichever came first.

'Andi!' Dad yelled over his shoulder. 'What are you waiting for? Come on in.'

I went in.

I'd forgotten that the hallway was bigger than our old kitchen. The sitting room was practically a cathedral. Our sofa would totally disappear in it. The ceiling was quadruple Mum's height!

Wow.

'Come upstairs to the bedrooms!' Mum said.

Dad and I followed her up.

'This will be your bedroom, Andi.' Mum threw open one door.

My room! I tried not to look too excited as I gazed into the cavernous space. I could paint it whatever colour I liked. I could put posters up on the walls. And I didn't have to sleep on a trundle bed, covering my ears while Mum and Dad snored for England.

'And if' – Mum took a deep breath – 'WHEN Bernardo comes, this will be *his* room.' She turned the knob of the door opposite mine. It wouldn't turn.

'Let me try,' Dad said. But he couldn't open the

door either. 'It's stuck. Don't do anything; I'll just go and get a screwdriver.' He ran down the stairs.

'Maybe we just have to push it,' I said, leaning my shoulder on the door and pushing. The door swung open. 'See!'

'What was that sound?' Mum said.

It was a gentle rumble like traffic approaching.

And then there was a thunderclap.

And then the ceiling fell down.

7

Bernardo

I knew, the moment I saw the envelope inside the mailbox.

I knew, even before I saw the logo.

I knew before I tore it open.

I had wished upon the wishing stone so I knew.

But still my hands shook as I read the letter and tears sprang to my eyes. I had waited for this moment my whole life. But alongside the joy, I felt a stab of fear.

'What is it, Nardo? Is it from London?' Uncle called from where he sat, a newspaper on his lap. He reached across and switched off the stereo just as Auntie's favourite singer, Tom Jones, was about to belt out another chorus.

In the sudden silence, I held the letter out to him.

Uncle spotted the official logo at the top of the page. 'Oh my God.' He stood up and took the letter from me, holding it close to his nose as if the writing had suddenly become too small to read.

'Why did you turn off the stereo?' Auntie appeared at the kitchen door.

Uncle just looked at her, still holding the letter up to his face.

'What? What is it?' Auntie Sofia bustled over and read over Uncle's shoulder. 'OH MY GOD!' She snatched it from Uncle and read it again, her mouth wide open.

It was from the British Home Office. Granting me permission to live in London.

Uncle and Auntie both looked so dumbfounded I could have laughed. But I felt dizzy, the booming of my heart filled my ears and the sweat on my back felt icy even though it was boiling hot.

'Oh, darling, this is fantastic!' Auntie hugged the letter and bounced with excitement, all her bumps jiggling like jelly.

'London, here you come!' Uncle grinned so wide his face seemed split in half. 'At last!'

I smiled down at them, a warmth spreading swiftly from my tummy to the tuft of hair on the top of my head which always brushed against the ceiling. A walking feather duster, Auntie called me. 'Look at those ceilings,' she said. 'No cobwebs in sight, thanks to our Nardo.'

My fingers closed around the wishing stone in my pocket. *She wanted you to have it. It was her dying wish.* I tried not to wonder why Gabriela would leave me the stone. I tried not to remember Mad Nena's last words. *Be careful what you wish for.*

In my fingers, the stone suddenly flared with a burning heat. I pulled my hand away just as both Uncle and Auntie reached up to embrace me.

Uncle frowned. 'Nardo? What's wrong?'

Auntie stared at my face, her lips forming a round 'o'. The letter fell from her hands.

I opened my mouth to reply. *Nothing. Nothing at all. I'm so happy. At last. At last.*

But my lips had turned to granite. I heard a strange grating noise, like an old gate sagging open. It was coming from the back of my throat where a pebble had lodged, trapping all the words. *Gragrrgh,* I said through solid jaws.

Then there was something on my shoulder. Something big and round and rough. And damp. It was so *damp*.

It grew heavier and heavier and heavier. *Crushingly* heavy. Bending me down, down, down. A boulder. A mountain. What was it?

It was the Earth.

The Earth? Had I gone crazy?

I stood there like Atlas, oceans and rivers sending trickles of water down my arm, forests like sandpaper against my skin, mountains poking into the nape of my neck.

Too heavy, too heavy. I couldn't . . . It slipped down my shoulder and I could have cried out as the mountain peaks jabbed hard against my skin. My muscles ached as I tried not to buckle under the weight, my hands scrabbling to hold on to it, the dirt grinding under my fingernails.

Mustn't drop it. *Mustn't drop the Earth.*

Then Auntie screamed and everything went black.

When I opened my eyes, Auntie and Uncle were leaning over me, their faces squeezed into frowns.

Behind them, Jabby bobbed around like a balloon. Jabby? I shut my eyes and opened them again. But Jabby wasn't here a moment ago when . . . when . . .

'Oh thank the Lord, he's awake,' Auntie said, crossing herself.

'Jabby?' I murmured.

Jabby pressed forward. He had his backpack over

his shoulder like he'd just walked in. 'You OK, Nards?' he asked.

'I'm fine,' I said, slowly becoming aware that the thing digging into the back of my neck was not the Earth but the hard wooden arm of the settee. I touched my shirt, which had been soaking from the dripping oceans. It was dry.

'Do you think we should call a doctor?' Uncle said.

I looked out of the window. From where I lay I could just see the yellow haloes of the coconut trees as the sun set. Tricycle cabs clattered on the street outside and the odour of stir-frying garlic, onions and tomatoes wafted in from Sister Len-Len's next door.

But just a moment ago I had the Earth on my shoulder, warm and damp and trickling. Was it a dream? Or was I going mad?

'Nards.' Jabby dropped the backpack on the floor and knelt down next to me. 'I think you ought to say something else, otherwise we might think you've cracked your coconut.'

I pushed him away.

'Don't crowd him, Henry, he needs air.' Auntie nudged Jabby on the shoulder.

Jabby's real name is Henry but when he caught basketball fever he adopted the name Jabbar – as in

Kareem Abdul-Jabbar, a star from the olden days who scored more points, blocked more shots, won more prizes than any other player in his league.

'Please, Sister Sofia, don't call me Henry, call me Jabbar!' Jabby said automatically. 'Have you heard of Kareem Abdul-Jabbar, the basketball legend? He—'

'You suddenly fell, Nardo,' Uncle interrupted, watching me with serious eyes. 'It was a business getting you into the chair. You weigh a ton. How do you feel?'

I felt fine. I pushed myself up on my elbow and ran a hand across the ache at the back of my neck.

'When did Jabby come in?'

'I was hungry so I came over,' Jabby said with a mischievous glint in his eyes.

'HENRY!' Auntie glared at him. 'Stay away from my fridge!'

'You were out for only two or three minutes.' Uncle stared at me thoughtfully.

Auntie frowned. 'How do you feel now, Nardo? Victor, we ought to take him to a doctor—'

'No, no.' I got slowly to my feet. 'I . . . I'm fine.'

'Nardo!'

Auntie's voice echoed somewhere in the back of my brain. Her mouth opened and closed but all I could hear were distant murmurs, like I was swimming under water. Uncle's face swam up close. I shook my head. The walls of the sitting room seemed to press inwards.

I squinted at Jabby.

He looked shiny, as if a spotlight was picking out every curve of his broad shoulders, every line of his laughing face. *I made a wish, Jabby*, I wanted to say. *I made a wish on the wishing stone and it came true. I'm going to London!*

Uncle caught my eye from over Jabby's shoulder. He shook his head silently and held his finger up to his lips.

Jabby grinned, unaware.

Uncle cleared his throat. 'We need to discuss that ... uh ... letter, yes? You mustn't um tell ... you know ...'

'Yes, yes, Uncle.' I gave him a hard look. 'I understand.' *They didn't want me to tell Jabby about London. They didn't want anyone to know that I was going to leave town.*

Uncle gave me a tight-lipped smile.

I sighed. 'Uncle, I need to go outside. I need some air.'

'But you're not well.' Auntie twisted her fingers into a knot.

'I'll be OK,' I said firmly. 'Come on, Jabs.' I turned to leave, thrusting my hands into my pockets.

My hand closed around it again. Hard and flat and round. It was still warm.

The wishing stone.

8
Andi

I only went to the Philippines that one time with Mum and Dad when I was just three years old.

And though I have a vague recollection of the heat and the itch of mosquito bites, the rest is a blur.

What I do remember is the earthquake.

It was the middle of the night and I was lying next to Mum. It must have been a small bed because we were cuddled up close together, sweat breaking out wherever skin touched. There was an electric fan. A pink nylon mosquito net hung from the ceiling, its edges tucked under our mattress. Dad had come with us to the Philippines but I couldn't remember him being in the same bed. He must have slept elsewhere.

I was wakeful, staring up at the pretty ripples that the electric fan blew into the mosquito net as it rotated. From the open window a street lamp bathed everything in a warm yellow glow.

Suddenly the bed began to sway, like we were on a giant swing. The motion swung me easily over the side of the bed, where the mosquito netting caught me like a trapeze safety-net.

I lay there and screamed.

Dad suddenly appeared in the doorway yelling, 'Mary Ann! Mary Ann! The baby!'

Mum groped around the edge of the bed like she was searching for a lost remote control. I screamed until she found me.

Then Dad grabbed me and we all stumbled outside in the middle of the night, in our pyjamas.

Mum never took me to the Philippines again.

Every two years or so she would go and visit Bernardo for a few weeks, and Dad and I would go off to Cornwall or somewhere like that.

Mum said the money she saved not buying me plane tickets meant she could visit Bernardo more often. Fair enough. I guess.

So that was the one time I met Bernardo in the flesh. He must have been six years old.

But I don't remember *him*.

All I remember is the earthquake.

9
Bernardo

The first time I saw the wishing stone, I wasn't actually looking at it.

I was thirteen and in my first year at the Sacred Heart Academy. It was nestled between Gabriela's breasts, which swelled boldly from her unbuttoned school blouse.

'Don't, idiot,' Jabby had whispered. 'She's trouble. Stop staring.'

'I'm not staring,' I lied.

Jabby was tall enough to pass for a senior but I was still small enough to be mistaken for a grader. Gabriela at sixteen was a full-grown woman in a tight school uniform. I couldn't help just . . . looking.

'Move it, Nardo.' Jabby pushed me roughly in the back and I stumbled past Gabriela and her gang. She threw back her neck and laughed.

I wasn't sure what the joke was but I smiled at her.

The Sacred Heart Academy was run by nuns from a German order, with a list of school rules and regulations that was long and precise. Boys had to have their hair cut around their ears. Girls with long hair had to tie their hair back in pony tails. Girls with short hair had to pin back their fringes. Shirts had to be buttoned up to the neck, despite the tropical heat. And the girls' regulation navy skirts had to be one and a half inches above the middle of the knee. No jewellery was allowed.

But Gabriela wore her dark hair down to her waist and never tied it back. She hitched her skirt all the way up to mid-thigh. And around her neck she wore the wishing stone on a chain.

At the time of course I knew nothing about it, just like I knew nothing about Gabriela.

So when she smiled at me, I thought it would be rude not to smile back.

'Idiot!' Jabby said again, between his teeth. He turned and walked away.

Gabriela stroked the stone on her chest. 'Do you know what this is?'

'No.' I looked up at her. Her lips were soft petals. Jabby paused, listening.

'It's a wishing stone. You need only think about something you really, really want and there it is!'

'Really?' I wished I didn't sound quite so eager.

'Really. Would you like to make a wish, little boy?'

'He's not a little boy,' Jabby said. I wondered at the anger in his voice. 'He's the same age as me.'

'Oh?' Gabriela's lashes swept briefly over her eyes, like she was considering the information carefully. Then she bent low and gazed into mine. 'But you are so sweet and tiny.'

'Come on, Nardo.' Jabby grabbed my arm and tugged. 'Let's go.'

'Nardo?' Gabriela smiled. 'As in Bernardo?

I nodded.

'Like the giant?'

'No. I mean, yes.'

Gabriela clapped her hands. 'How funny!'

'Come,' Jabby grunted. But my feet seemed to have taken root. My eyes were locked with Gabriela's. Even if I had wanted to, I couldn't move.

'Listen, Nardo, do you want to wish upon my stone?' She was still talking as if I was one of the kids in Grade Two but I didn't mind.

I shook my head.

She pouted, but I could tell that she was only pretending to be disappointed. 'Go on. Why don't you wish yourself taller. Like your namesake!'

She unhooked the chain from around her neck and

the stone slid silkily onto her hand. It seemed to gleam in her palm. I couldn't take my eyes off it.

'Go on,' she was whispering now.

I reached out.

'*Nardo!*'

Jabby forced me away by the shoulders. 'Sorry, Gabriela, we're late for algebra.'

And Gabriela laughed as Jabby frog-marched me away.

'Well,' she said. 'Maybe next time.'

10
Andi

When Auntie Sofia rang, Mum screamed.
If my ears hadn't been cabled to an MP3
player, she would probably have shattered my eardrums.

She screamed some more, little needle shrieks,
clutching the phone to her head. There were tears
streaming down her cheeks. She wiped at the
tears with the back of her other hand, smearing her
mascara.

Was she screaming because she was happy or was
she screaming because she was sad? It was always
hard to tell with Mum.

She looked at me, her nose dripping ever so
slightly. She covered the mouthpiece with a trembling
hand. 'It's Bernardo, Andi . . . Bernardo!'

Bernardo! My stomach clenched. Poor Bernardo.
What could have happened?

'What about him, Mum? Is he all right?'

Mum was speaking into the mouthpiece again.

'How soon can he come? Yes, yes, Sofia, I've always

said if the papers came through, he should come over as soon as possible.'

As soon as possible? It wasn't bad news, it was good news! My stomach unclenched and I rushed to Mum's side.

Mum's eyes were closed, mouth moving in a quick prayer of thanks. She covered the mouthpiece but when she spoke she could hardly get the words out. 'Andi, Bernardo's got his papers. He's coming to England! He'll be here *next week!*'

I gaped. Bernardo. Here. Next week.

It was a miracle.

I pulled the earphones out of my ears so fast they made little popping noises. I threw my arms around Mum and she buried her face in my shoulder, soaking my T-shirt. The phone, which was still pressed to her ear, made a hard knob against my neck.

I fished my mobile phone out of my pocket. I should text Dad the good news! I began to thumb a message.

Mum was laughing and crying at the same time now. 'Yes, yes, of course. Go ahead, Sofia, I'm so happy, you can say anything to me right now. Tell me the roof has fallen down, or the pig has escaped, or the . . .'

Then Mum straightened up so suddenly, her head almost banged me in the jaw. She grabbed my wrist as if her life depended on it and her tan drained away to a mottled grey.

'WHAT?'

Mum's eyes were platters.

This was some other kind of news.

'What?' she said again.

'What?' I said like a stupid echo. 'What's wrong?'

'SOFIA!' Her face was a mixture of fury and – what was it? Horror? 'Oh my God, Sofia.'

She covered her mouth with one hand, strangled noises coming out of the back of her throat.

Auntie's voice crackled tinnily over the line. 'Hello? Hello, Mary Ann? Can you hear me?'

Mum dropped the phone into her lap.

'What's the matter, Mum? What's wrong?'

She turned away and collapsed on the sofa, hands covering her face for the longest time.

When she spoke, her voice was hoarse, like she'd suddenly developed a sore throat.

'It's Bernardo,' she said.

'What about Bernardo?'

There was anguish in the look she gave me.

'Bernardo is TALL.'

11
Bernardo

'Hello? Hello, Mary Ann? Can you hear me?' Auntie frowned and stared at the telephone as if she could fix the connection just by looking.

I wished now that we had kept that promise. We should have told Ma that I was still growing. We could have told her as soon as I hit seven foot. Seven foot didn't sound as shocking as eight foot. Somehow it seemed still . . . normal.

But when I suggested we tell Ma, Auntie just burst out in exasperation, '*Jesus Mary Joseph!* Nardo, your ma is a nurse. A nurse! She is a scientist, not a believer. She will spit on the soul of Bernardo Carpio and then what? Where will San Andres be?'

So we didn't say anything.

And I grew.

And now . . . eight foot. It was impossible. A point of no return.

Like everyone else, Jabby and I liked to hang out

in the street just before the sun set, when the temperature cooled suddenly and the low sun didn't burn.

We leaned on the gate and watched the world go by. Or shot hoops through the basketball goal nailed to the telephone pole outside Jabby's house.

Well. Jabby shot hoops. I watched. Occasionally, when the ball swooped the wrong way, I reached up and tipped the ball into the basket.

The cooler temperatures drew people out of their houses and street vendors tried to press them into buying pork barbecue, fish balls, steamed corn, and sweet bananas fried in crispy wonton wrappers. Passenger tricycles rattled slowly up and down the street, casting for fares.

Inevitably, Old Tibo would wave from his shop opposite my house. 'Nardo, Nardo!' His dog, Flash Gordon, always gave a high-pitched yelp, as if to add his own greeting.

Sister Len-Len always made sure to catch my eye from where she fried garlic peanuts in her stall. 'Hello, Nardo.'

Salim never failed to slow his tricycle cab alongside. 'Nardo. How are you?'

'Fine, Brother Salim,' I would say and Salim

would gun his motor by way of salute and drive off.

It sometimes got to Jabbar.

'I'm fine too!' he used to yell. 'I'm really healthy!'

I tried to apologize but Jabby shrugged it off with a joke. 'It's not easy being best friends with Mister "Saviour of the World",' he would say, striking a tragic pose.

'I'm not!' I would laugh. But Jabby was right.

Only four years earlier, San Andres got into the Book of World Records for the hundreds of teeny tiny tremors that shook it every day.

On the World Records website, the entry says: *The village of San Andres holds the distinction of reporting hundreds of earthquakes a day since seismologists began measuring the tremors in the 1940s. It is said the tremors are only a rehearsal for an earthquake so massive it will probably level the village when it finally comes.* Above the article was the headline: *The Land of Rock and Roll.*

There was a picture in pen and ink of a giant standing between two cliff sides, muscles bulging as he strained to push them apart. The caption said: *Villagers await the return of a giant of legend named Bernardo Carpio. Folklore has it that only the giant can truly save the village from destruction.*

So imagine what a big deal it was when people discovered a boy amongst them named Bernardo who was shooting up like a giant bamboo.

And imagine what they thought when, as the boy grew, the rock and roll dwindled to a full stop.

And then imagine how they would feel if they knew their saviour was about to leave them to their fate.

'First we tell her the good news,' Auntie said firmly. 'We tell her you're coming. And then she will be so happy, surely, she won't be too upset about your height.'

'OK,' I said. But I was dubious.

'Why don't we explain?' Uncle said. 'Tell her about Bernardo Carpio? About what everyone in San Andres says?'

Of course, we didn't encourage the gifts and the thank-yous. But we didn't discourage them either.

I didn't feel like Bernardo Carpio. I didn't feel like a *saviour*. A saviour wouldn't have stiff joints and lower back pain and aching knees because of his ungainly size.

But I looked at Auntie and Uncle and Old Tibo

and all the people of San Andres and I wanted to be who they thought I was.

Uncle opened a thesaurus to look for synonyms for the words 'tall' and 'grow'. 'How about "mature"?' he said. 'Let's just casually say that Bernardo's really become . . . mature.'

'She's not stupid, Victor.' Auntie frowned. 'Besides, the moment Bernardo steps off that plane, the game will be up. We must tell her the truth.'

So Auntie made the call.

It went very well at first as Auntie relayed the Home Office's miraculous change of mind. She beamed as Ma squawked with joy from the other side of the world.

And then she told her.

The phone stopped squawking.

'Hello? Mary Ann?' Auntie shook the telephone receiver.

'What is it?' Uncle reached for the phone but she brushed his hand away, listening intently and tapping the receiver with a long fingernail.

'What is she saying?' I asked. 'Let me speak to Ma.'

Auntie shook her head.

'Oh, I've had enough of this.' Uncle stood up and snatched the phone away.

Auntie immediately pressed the button and the distant drone of a dial tone sounded. 'I think we've lost the line,' she said.

Uncle glared at her and put the phone down.

'How did she take it?' I said anxiously.

Auntie's smile was as hard as plastic. 'I think she took it very well.'

12
Andi

Since the Phone Call, Mum's turned into a character from this book I read in English who one moment is nice-but-needy Dr Jekyll, the next is monstrous Mr Hyde.

So one moment Mum is walking on air because truly this was the dream she'd been working towards for years and years. Bernardo was coming to England. Hallelujah!

The next moment she's hunkered like someone waiting for the apocalypse. Unpacking the boxes, putting things away, cleaning the house like a demon. Grim.

Suddenly everything was Bernardo, Bernardo, Bernardo.

Bernardo coming to England eclipsed all Mum's plans. Sorting out the new house. Putting me in a new school. Settling me in. Everything.

The morning of my first day at Saint Sim's, I came downstairs to find her washing the tops of the doors.

'Honestly, Mum. Bernardo isn't going to inspect the tops of the doors.'

Mum looked down at me like I was the crazy one. 'Bernardo is *tall*.'

OK.

I tried to ask her *how* tall is Bernardo – six foot? Six foot two inches? She just clicked her tongue and complained that Auntie Sofia never took her seriously. That they should have said something.

But who cares if Bernardo is six foot tall? Loads of boys my age are beginning to shoot up. George McGregor at my old school was six foot tall, and boy was I glad to see the back of him, the jackass.

'I'll be off, Mum,' I said.

'I'll be down in a minute,' she said, totally forgetting to nag me to eat some breakfast. 'I'd better walk you to school since it's your first day.'

'Don't worry about me,' I said, moving quickly to the door. She didn't even pretend to try to get down from the stepladder. 'I'll just report to the school office. I can manage.'

Mrs Green said it before I could stop her.

'Class,' she said, 'this is Amandolina Jones.'

The class laughed like a pack of hyenas.

Right.

'It's *Andi*, actually,' I said. 'Andi with an *i*.'

But they were laughing too hard to hear me.

Mum said she chose the name Amandolina because one of her best friends was named Amandolina, and besides, Amandolina sounded musical. Musical? It sounded more like something with long pointy ears from *The Lord of the Rings*. Dad told me not to say stuff like that because I couldn't blame Mum for not realizing it was an odd name – she grew up on the other side of the world, how was she supposed to know? Sure. But *you*, Dad, should have known better. *You* grew up in London, *you* went to a London secondary school, *you* knew what London kids were like. But when I said this, Dad just said I was lucky they didn't name me Tiger Lily Mini-Ha-Ha.

Honestly.

When the class finished laughing, Mrs Green put me in a seat at the back of the classroom, next to a boy named Joe Beedle. Joe grinned at me so broadly, I was afraid one of the spots on his cheek would burst. I nodded at him. But I wasn't in the mood to make friends. All I wanted was to turn invisible.

Mrs Green was explaining something desperately

boring as she handed out some literacy sheets.

Joe took his sheet from the pile and held one out to me.

'Thanks,' I muttered, taking it. But he didn't let go.

He winked. 'Amandolina . . . love the name.'

'Yeah, thanks.' I tugged at the sheet but still he wouldn't let go.

'It's, like, got the word "doll" in it, yeah? AmanDOLLina?'

I glared at him. 'No it hasn't.'

'So why do you call yourself Andi?'

I pulled hard and there was a loud rip as the sheet tore in half. Heads turned in our direction.

'Andi . . . like undies . . . underwear . . . knickers? Maybe you should call yourself Knickers, yeah?' He laughed at his own lame joke.

Something white-hot exploded behind my eyes. Before Joe Beedle could withdraw, I had his wrist in my grip.

The thing is, you know, with all the basketball training, I'm really strong. Strong enough to shoot a ball into the hoop from the halfway line. Strong enough to break a stupid boy's wrist.

Of course I didn't break it. The only reason Joe started crying was because of the pain.

Wimp.

Mrs Green was totally suckered in by Joe Beedle's howling and refused to let me explain. She said I needed to learn the value of Patience and Restraint. So at the end of my first day at my new school, I had to sit in detention for an hour watching her get the *Times* sudoku wrong.

I should have been annoyed.

But I wasn't.

Because stuck to the notice board behind Mrs Green's head was a poster.

BASKETBALL, ANYONE?

Saint Simeon Souls Are **RECRUITING**!
Try-outs: Friday, 8.30 a.m., New Gym

13
Bernardo

'Come on.' Jabby adjusted the backpack on his shoulder and gestured for me to follow him down the side street.

He dribbled his ball, expertly avoiding the cracks in the asphalt as if he was running a gauntlet of defenders on a basketball court.

'Where are we going?'

'You'll see.'

The sun was turning into a red fist in the gathering dusk. I realized that we were approaching the new sports centre crouched at the end of the road, its dome bulging above the trees like an overturned coconut shell.

The sports centre, the Arena, had been in construction for ever. The first contractor had gone bust. The second contractor was jailed for some kind of bribery scam to do with building materials. The third contractor resigned, saying the whole thing needed to be rebuilt. It was on its fourth contractor now. And nothing ever seemed to be going on.

The flimsy temporary fencing was erected many years ago when construction began. I wouldn't be at all surprised if, under the layers of graffiti, the boards had rotted away to nothing. Above the original fence, the builders had added a few more courses of marine ply. It was now so high, even I couldn't see over it. *Trespassers Will Be Prosecuted*, the sign on top declared.

'What are we doing here, Jabs?'

Jabby put his fingers to his lips. 'Shh,' he whispered. And then he winked. He kicked a panel of graffiti and it swung open. A secret door.

Jabby tossed the basketball through the narrow gap and slipped in after it.

I hung back. 'It says trespassers will be—'

'There's never anybody here. Come on!'

I had to bend at the waist to get through the door. I followed Jabby into the Arena's back yard.

It was a mess. A mountain of gravel listed precariously in one corner and untidy stacks of concrete blocks were dotted haphazardly around the yard.

Bamboo scaffolding covered everything. What I could see of the dome had been whitewashed – but

71

the dark grey of concrete showed through the thin paint like a five o'clock shadow.

'There must be a security guard somewhere,' I muttered.

'There never is. I've been here loads of times. This way.' Jabby had not stopped. There was a door to one side. A fat padlock hung from the latch.

'We shouldn't be here.'

'Come on!' Jabs pulled at the padlock and it fell to the ground with a thick clunk. 'Follow me!'

I hunched low to enter the doorway into a dark, airless tunnel.

Jabby stood at the end of the tunnel, one shoe drumming impatiently on the floor. When I was safely through, he turned and marched into the darkness. He bounced the ball once or twice, sending echoes through the tunnel like gunshots.

'Jabby? I can't see anything.' I lumbered slowly after him, my fingers tracing a path on the rough concrete walls.

'Wait a minute.' Jabby's voice was distant and echoing. It sounded like he was somewhere above me, to the left. 'I'll be right back!'

I waited, staring into the murk.

The air was choked with construction dust but

there were other smells too – new wood, paint, cardboard and styrofoam.

Then, high above my head, the lights bloomed on like a hundred little suns.

I realized I was standing next to a basketball goal. It was made of transparent fibreglass, like the ones you see on TV. Nothing like the ones at the park which had warped badly after only one monsoon.

The net hanging from the hoop was red, white and blue, and so new the white bits glowed like Old Tibo's false teeth.

Beneath my feet, the floor was made of a yellow wood, shiny and smooth.

Tiers of red seats wound round and round and up and up to the high domed roof.

All this time I had assumed that the sports centre was nowhere near finished. I was wrong.

'Wow.' I turned. Jabby was slowly descending from wherever it was he'd switched on the lights, cradling his basketball like a baby, a big grin on his face. 'I had no idea.'

He flexed his shoulder muscles and pushed the ball into the sky. It arced high but I reached up at just the right moment and tipped it gently into the basket. It bounced on the yellow floor with a satisfying *thunk*.

Jabby caught it after the first bounce.

'Ace!'

It was the one move I could do on the basketball court. Jabby and I spent a lot of time practising variations of it. Under the basket. To the right. To the left. It wasn't *proper* basketball, but at least it was something we could do together, since with my big feet and my brittle knees, I couldn't run to save myself.

Jabby thunked the ball once or twice and released it from the free-throw line. *Swish*. It dropped neatly through the net. 'Not only is it finished, the Arena is all set to open. In two weeks!'

'Two weeks? But I haven't seen any posters. Shouldn't they be advertising?'

'They will – they're just sorting out some local teams for the exhibition game.' He stood on the three-point line and attempted another shot. He missed. The ball ricocheted off the hoop with a powerful *crack*.

Two weeks! I would be in London by then. I bit my lip.

Jabby grabbed the ball and turned to the backpack he had flung down on the end line.

'I brought you here for a reason.' His eyes sparkled as he unzipped his backpack.

'What?'

Jabbar cleared his throat, as if he was going to make an announcement over the public address system. 'My friend, I have gathered you here today to celebrate a momentous occasion.' He extracted a Mountain Men shirt just like his, holding it out to me delicately, like some kind of sacred offering.

'What?' I stared at it.

'A gift, Nardo. It's a gift.' Jabbar pushed the shirt into my hands. 'A Mountain Men shirt. An official invitation to join the most amazing basketball team on this side of the South China Sea, with the most amazing team captain on this earth. Me.'

I couldn't speak. My Adam's apple suddenly felt like the size of a basketball. 'I . . . thanks, Jabby.'

'You're welcome.' He looked around the stadium, pleased with himself. 'Isn't this great?'

'Jabs . . .' I stared at the shirt. Jabby must have had it made specially. Maybe by Timbuktu, who had to make all my clothes because nothing in the shops fitted me.

'Come on, Nards, try it on!'

I frowned. 'Jabby, I can't join the Mountain Men. It would be a disaster. Look at me. I'm so clumsy. I can't even run . . .'

'And that's not all.' Jabby was not listening. 'You know the Arena's supposed to recruit local teams for the big opening?'

I nodded.

'We're it!'

'What do you mean?'

'The Mountain Men. They picked us!'

'Wow, congratulations!' I should have been jumping up and down at our good fortune but I was still trying to process his invitation. I loved basketball. But I would be a complete embarrassment to the Mountain Men. I would be a joke. How could Jabby even consider . . . ?

'And guess what the other team is called.'

'What?'

'The Giant Killers.'

'*The Giant Killers?*'

I stiffened.

'They requested to play us specially. Nardo, people will be coming from miles around to watch us play.' Jabby grinned. 'And the Arena said they would give us a share of ticket receipts. We're going to be rich!'

I understood now. 'You mean, they will be coming for miles to see the Giant Killers try to slay a real *giant*.'

'No, that's not it.' Jabby's brown skin paled. 'Wait, you don't understand.'

I whirled around and headed blindly for the tunnel. 'Nardo!'

I stopped and threw the shirt back at him. It lay like a puddle at his feet.

'You just needed me for ticket sales. You don't need a player, you need a *sideshow*. You only want me as the team *freak*.'

And Jabby said nothing.

So I knew it was true.

14
Andi

I hope Mum realizes how awesome I've been about the whole brother business. I couldn't imagine any of the kids at my school being so relaxed about suddenly acquiring a sibling. Go ahead, World, bring on the long-lost relatives.

For the first time since the day Mum told me we were moving house, I was feeling buoyant. Saint Sim's had a basketball team and the basketball team was recruiting. I had my own room and lived in a proper-sized house instead of a rabbit hutch. My brother was finally coming home. Everything was good.

I practically skipped up the steps to our front door. Mum should be relieved to hear she didn't need to feel guilty about the basketball any more. I glanced at the time on my mobile. It was four o'clock. Mum would be home. She shouldn't have to leave for work for a couple of hours yet. She wouldn't be leaving until six and Dad should be back soon from the day shift. Which was a reversal. Two weeks before, Mum was doing the day shift and Dad the night shift. They barely overlapped some weeks. It amazed me that they could still remember each other's names.

'I'm home, Mum!' I yelled as I pushed through into the hall. Mum had hung a butterfly mobile that Auntie Sofia had sent years ago near the stairs. Nice. I hummed as I made my way up to my room.

'Mum!' Maybe she'd decided to wash the ceilings as well, or polish the grass in the garden – she was in that kind of mood.

I opened the door to my room.

'Oh, Andi, I didn't hear you.'

Mum was on the stepladder, hanging curtains.

It was a heartbeat before I realized what had jarred as I walked into the room.

On the floor next to my bed, two mattresses had been laid side by side.

The wardrobe door sagged open, and all the clothes I had carefully put away were now piled high on my bed.

Oh Holy Mother of God.

Mum looked at me and I could see guilt etched on her face.

'It's not what you think.'

I shook my head. 'I don't know what to think.'

'You know, Bernardo is quite big, so I've put two single mattresses together to make up his bed. It's temporary.'

'Temporary?' And then suddenly it dawned on me.

After the ceiling fell down, Bernardo's room was a ruin. The ceiling had to be rebuilt, the walls repainted, the carpet relaid.

You could see right up into the attic rafters through the gaping hole in the ceiling. There was a smell like wet towels that had not dried properly and I thought I heard squeaking up in the hole. Gross.

'It was damp to begin with,' Dad had said after the crash. 'We knew that from the survey.'

And now there was a bed on my floor.

'Look, Bernardo will share your room until his ceiling is mended.'

'When?'

'When what?'

'When is the ceiling going to be mended?'

Mum smiled a bright, fake smile. 'Soon. I'm working on it. We have to sort out the insurance. And it takes time to find a good builder.'

'He can't share my room,' I said. 'He's a boy.'

'He's your brother.'

'But I don't know him.'

'Oh, try to be hospitable,' Mum said. 'Filipinos are the most hospitable people in the world.'

'But I'm English.'

'You're half Filipino.'

'I've only been to the Philippines once in my life.'

'And you loved it!'

'I can't speak Tagalog.'

'His English is very good!'

'Why can't he sleep in the living room? Or how about *your* room?'

Mum frowned at me. 'Well, I was going to put him in the living room at first but then I thought, Bernardo is sixteen, he needs privacy.'

'What about *my* privacy?'

'You're both teenagers!' Mum said. 'You have so much in common!'

Brilliant.

15
Bernardo

There was a humming and the bed shivered as if it had suddenly been nudged awake.

I sat up.

Earthquake?

The bed trembled again.

But no.

It was the cellphone on vibration alert under my pillow.

It was just a text message.

I pulled the phone out. The little screen flashed blue in the darkness.

The number had a +44 country code for the UK. It was Mama.

gud night nardo. cant w8 to c u.

I texted back: night ma. c u soon.

I lay back again, awake now. Shadows huddled on the ceiling. Only a few more days and I would be on a plane to London. But in the pit of my stomach, angry teeth nibbled.

You don't need a player, you need a sideshow. You only want me as the team freak.

· I clenched my fists. Jabby might as well have punched me in the face. How could he use his best friend like some sort of *thing* to barter at the market? *How could he?*

He didn't know, did he, that I was about to leave? I imagined it. Jabby turning up at the front door like he always did, touching Auntie's hand to his forehead before calling for me over her shoulder.

Nardo! Nardo!

And Auntie smiling sadly at him.

Nardo isn't here! He went to London.

And him gazing down at Auntie, jaw dropping in shock.

London?

I'm sorry. We couldn't tell anyone. He's not coming back.

And Jabby would be sorry. Sorry. Sorry.

My face was suddenly wet and my heart seized with guilt.

Jabby would be sorry but so would San Andres.

Everybody would be sorry to see me go.

And frightened.

Because what if the earthquakes returned?

83

Remorse suddenly had me by the throat. Was I about to bring calamity to my village? How could I even think of leaving? What if something happened?

I rubbed my eyes. No. No. No. Nothing was going to happen. The whole Bernardo Carpio thing, it was just a legend, wasn't it? Nobody really believed it, surely. I laughed. But all I made was a hollow, rusty sound.

Mad Nena made things worse of course, with her crazy, apocalyptic declarations.

But it was Old Tibo who had made everybody believe. Poor Tibo with all his stories of gods and giants.

Whenever I went to Tibo for a haircut, the old man greeted me like a VIP. When I tried to touch his hand to my forehead to show my respect, he waved me off like he didn't deserve it. And then he ceremoniously took mine and touched the back of my hand to his forehead. It was so wrong, an old man giving respect to a boy. His dog, Flash Gordon, fluttered around my knees like a little bird, he was so overjoyed to see me.

Every man and boy in the village had experienced their first haircut at Tibo's ancient hands. It was like a benediction. Tibo was the oldest person in the barrio; his family had run a barbershop on the same spot on our road for almost a century.

The year Ma came to visit with little Amandolina and Uncle William, when the big earthquake hit, we all rushed out into the streets in our nightclothes, Amandolina in her father's arms, me in Uncle Victor's, and Ma and Auntie clutching each other like young girls. I remember hearing the sharp crackle of windows shattering like popcorn, the high wail which at first I thought was a fire truck's siren but turned out to be screaming as people ran out into the street. And I remember Old Tibo weeping as he fell on his knees in the rubble. The earthquake had shaken his barbershop into kindling.

'Why, God? *Why?*'

Much later, when I was older, Auntie told me that it was not the first time Old Tibo's shop had been levelled by an earthquake.

The first time was many, many years ago, before Auntie was born, before most people now living in the village can remember. That time, the earthquake had struck while Tibo, his young wife and baby son were inside the shop.

That time, the tremors had been stronger, levelling

a chapel and the municipal hall. A few miles away, the hillside had yawned open and swallowed a schoolhouse, just like that. The seabed thrust giant waves onto the shore. A fishing village drowned.

Tibo was pulled out of the wreckage of his shop after twenty-four hours. He broke both his legs and a hip – but at least he was alive.

But both his wife and son were crushed to death.

16
Andi

We pulled into the school car park. The new gym sat on a fat cushion of mist.

Mum frowned and checked the clock on the Toyota's dashboard. 'I thought you said the trials were at eight o'clock? There's nobody here—'

'Eight-thirty,' I said, kissing the air next to her cheek and jumping out before she'd even finished her sentence. 'I wanted to get here early.' I ran into the gym, basketball under one arm, ignoring her squeal of protest.

The gym was pretty snazzy; it was so new it had yet to absorb the odour of socks and sweat and trainers, the default aroma of any secondary school gym.

I came early so I could warm up.

No. I lie.

I came early because I couldn't wait a minute longer. I was so excited, the butterflies in my stomach had morphed into monster ostriches.

There was an arctic gale blowing through the gap

between the double doors but I shrugged my tracksuit off anyway, I was that eager. On impulse, I had worn the Chicago Bulls basketball kit Dad got me on eBay. It was the first time I'd worn it and it felt crispy on my thighs.

But what if they took one look at me and said, 'Sorry, you're too short'?

The thought sent the ostriches galumphing. Stop thinking. Get going. Shoot some hoops.

I threw my stuff on a bench and ran out onto the court, dribbling the ball low as if a defender was already sweating over me.

OK, this is the thing about me and basketball: I may be small and I could be faster . . . but I never miss.

I. Never. Miss.

It's some kind of weight-versus-strength-versus-balance thing. I just don't miss. I shoot and the ball swishes through the basket. Hook shot. Set shot. Turn-around-jump shot. Lay-up. Under the basket. From the free-throw line. And even way, way out, from the three-point line.

It all goes in.

Swish.

Swish.

Swish.

I'd shot twenty in a row before the sound of the gym doors creaking open made me turn round to meet whoever it was – the coach? My new team-mates? Heart booming, teeth shredding my bottom lip, I wondered if I looked like an idiot in the Chicago Bulls kit, like I'd dressed up all posh for a jeans-and-T-shirt party. Suddenly I wished I'd worn my plain old Nike sweats instead.

The heavy double doors swung open slowly and a boy shouldered his way in, one arm wrapped around a large kit bag, the other dragging a net sack full of basketballs. Our eyes met and then both of us looked at the other from top to toe. Oh Holy Mother of God, he was wearing a Chicago Bulls kit too. I felt a blush start up in my cheeks and spread to my forehead and ears like a rash.

The boy pointed at the *No Entry Unless Authorized* sign on the door. 'Uh, you can't play here, we've got basketball trials scheduled for eight-thirty.' The stubby dreads on his head bounced like coiled springs.

'I'm here for the trials,' I said, hating that my whole face was now radiating more heat than a radiator. I probably looked like a well-boiled lobster. With freckles. 'Are you the coach?'

The boy put the kit bag down, let go of the sack, and folded his arms across his chest, looking me up and down. 'There's no coach. Just me. My name's Rocky. I'm the team captain.'

He was tall, probably six foot two, maybe more. I had to bend backwards from the waist to look up at him. He had biceps like boulders.

He stared at his shoes. 'Listen, I'm sorry but . . .'

'My name's Andi,' I said. 'Andi with an *i*. I started at Saint Sim's two days ago. My family just moved here. Near the hospital.'

'Ah,' the boy said. 'That explains everything.'

'Explains what?'

He smiled and scuffed the floor with his feet. Which were huge. I could probably swim in his Converses. 'Well, it's just that . . .'

I tried to relax. 'Oh, well. I know. I'm really small. But you've only got to see me play . . .'

'No, no.' Rocky's tan seemed to darken. Was he blushing too? 'It's . . . well, I've got to tell you now, before anyone else arrives. You've got it wrong.'

I closed one eye and peered up at him. What was he on about?

'Andi . . . it is Andi, isn't it?'

I nodded.

'Andi, it's great you're here but . . . you're new to the school so you had no reason to know . . .'

'No reason to know what?'

There was real sorrow in his doggy brown eyes. 'The Souls. It's a *boys'* team.'

For the first time in my life I wanted to be even smaller than I was. I wanted to shrink away until I disappeared.

'But your poster said: "Basketball, *anyone*",' I mumbled. 'And Saint Sim's is a mixed school – surely there's a boys' *and* a girls' . . .'

Rocky sucked his teeth and stepped closer, as if he wanted to do something sympathetic like pat me on the head.

'It's *boys only*. I'm sorry but you can't join the team. There isn't a girls' basketball team but there's a girls' netball team. How about—'

But I didn't wait to hear more. I grabbed my stuff from the bench, picked up my ball and ran.

17
Bernardo

'How is our Bernardo?' Tibo always asked when I came in for a haircut.

He meant Bernardo Carpio, of course.

'I'm fine,' I mumbled as he produced a footstool. I had to sit on the low stool so that he could cut my hair without the help of a ladder. I was never going to be small enough to sit on the barbering chairs that could lean back, move up and move down.

'Now, look. Up in the sky. What do you see?' Tibo would say.

'Nothing, sir. I see nothing,' I murmured resignedly.

'Precisely.' Old Tibo pulled his clippers out. 'So many millions of sins pushing the Heavens further and further away. Tragic.'

And then, as he cut my hair, he recited the story.

When Time began, people had no use for churches, nor did they pray. There was no need. Heaven sat low over the Earth, leaning gently against the tops of the coconut trees. Thus gods lived and walked amongst men – indeed many fell in love with mortals and married them.

The offspring of these mixed marriages were the giants, who looked human but were of a magical size. They may not have been gods but they were immortal – unlike the human side of their families.

As time passed, humankind grew older and wilier and innocence was lost and life became a matter of what one could get away with. The accumulated sins of man began to push up against the Heavens, pushing it higher and higher and further and further away until one day the gods were amazed to see that the Earth was just a distant green patch under the clouds beneath them.

The giants were confronted with a difficult choice: to live with their heavenly parents in the sky, or step down to Earth to live with their mortal families.

Many stayed in Heaven. But who could bear to be parted from his or her mother? The ones with human mothers returned to Earth.

So Heaven rose beyond the atmosphere and the giants who had chosen to stay leaped down to Earth to make their lives amongst ordinary men.

And they were happy.

But only while their mothers were alive.

Their mothers eventually passed away, as mortals do.

Their neighbours, who previously had shown no sign of ill will, suddenly turned against them. They massed in small paramilitaries and attacked the giants, burning their homes, destroying their crops, and driving them out of their villages.

Hurt and disappointed, the giants filtered out across the world, some stepping over oceans in search of other lands, others simply lying down in their grief, covering themselves with forest and rock and becoming part of the landscape.

'Do you really think that's a bamboo thicket sighing in the wind?' Old Tibo would put the clippers in his left hand to wag his right finger. 'Do you really think that's the monsoon howling? Do you really think that geology had a hand in carving that hill into the shape of a man's body?'

'No, sir,' I'd say, bowing my head.

'Giants! That's what they are. Just giants. As for earthquakes – an earthquake is nothing but a giant's shudder.'

This was my cue to ask the question I asked every time. 'Why would a giant shudder?'

'Regret, of course.' Old Tibo would shake his head sadly. 'All giants regret that they had to leave Heaven to be with their mortal mothers.'

The cellphone shuddered on the bed again. My eyes flew open. What time was it? I snatched the phone up.

But its little window remained dark.

Then it shook again.

It was not the phone.

It was the bed.

The wall.

The room.

Mama's picture on the wall tilted slowly to the right.

Earthquake.

Part Two

Mind the Gap

1
Andi

He had to crouch to get through the double doors.

And suddenly it was as if the crowd in Terminal 3 had turned into a sea of eyeballs, all swiftly rotated in our direction.

He was massive.

No, not massive, because he actually looked *slight*, if you could call a giant slight.

Slight like it would take a tiny gust to blow him over.

Slight like a long straw, all air and no structure.

Slight like an empty suit dangling from a hanger. A very *long* suit.

His shoulders were round and he was stooped.

Everything about him was lanky, his arms, his legs, his hair. Who cut his hair? It was *horrible*, chopped around his ears like a jigsaw. And don't get me started on the suit, made of some kind of *shiny* nylon, and the tie that hung like it had been pasted on with Velcro.

On his feet he wore some deeply ugly sandals with *black* socks.

The other passengers emerging from the doors flowed past him like a fast-moving stream as he made his way towards us, walking like his legs were tree trunks that he had to uproot with every step.

His face was all angles, like the bones had grown all wrong, his cheekbones jutting, too sharp for a boy's face.

Then when he spoke . . . oh, that voice!

He sounded like he was underwater. He sounded like he had the treble turned off. He sounded like Dad's prehistoric CD Walkman with a flat battery.

And yep. He was *tall*.

I mean, did Mum actually think she was preparing me to meet this . . . this GIRAFFE . . . by bleating 'he's tall' every few minutes?

Lame. Lame. LAME.

2
Bernardo

Ma leaped higher than a grasshopper in a paddy field to hug me. She just missed my shoulders and embraced me around the waist instead.

The Arrivals area shimmered behind the tears in my eyes and I squeezed her hard.

'Mama! Mama,' I murmured, my throat tight. Suddenly the worries that had plagued me since I got off the plane vanished. Losing my way, taking the wrong exit, picking the trolley with a sticky wheel – nothing mattered.

I was in London at last.

Uncle William was waving a long white streamer high in the air. I recognized him from the photos: pineapple hair cropped close to his head, freckles like orange dust all over his face. More tears welled in my eyes as I read the message written across the banner with a marker pen.

Welcome Home, Bernardo.

Remembering my manners, I bent low to touch Ma's hand to my forehead.

She grabbed my hand and cradled it against her cheek, whispering in Tagalog, 'Oh, my son. My baby. At last. At last.'

Uncle William came forward, rolling the streamer into a scroll. He gave me a quick hug.

'Welcome to London, Bernardo,' he said.

Instead of touching his hand to my forehead, I shook it firmly, hoping that my palms weren't sweaty. 'Once you're in England,' Auntie had admonished, 'do as the English do.'

But when I opened my mouth to speak, the English weighed my tongue down like a stone.

'I am glad you meet me.'

Uncle William smiled. 'Glad to meet you too,' he replied and I almost sagged with relief.

'I am fine, you are how?' I said.

Uncle William paused like he was adding up a complicated sum, but he just clapped me on the shoulder and answered my question as if everything was OK. 'I'm fine, Bernardo. Thank you for asking!'

Ma beamed up at me and continued to cling to my hand.

Where was Amandolina? There was no sign of my

sister in the airport crowd. Did she not come to meet me? Disappointment began to gnaw at my chest.

Ma turned to a freckled little boy in a Chicago Bulls jacket. 'Andi, aren't you going to say hello?'

The boy stared up at me open-mouthed. He was no higher than my hip bone.

Then he snapped his jaws together with a click.

'Hey, Bernardo,' he mumbled in a gruff voice, raising a hand in a half-salute while tracing a crack in the linoleum with the toe of his shoe.

I hesitated and then raised my hand too. 'Pleased you meet me?' I said, unsure.

The boy turned to Ma, his bottom lip thrust out, dark brows drawn together in a scowl. Uncle William frowned at the boy and Ma's grip on my hand tightened.

'Mum, why couldn't you just *tell* me?' he said in a soft voice.

'Andi!' Mum said. 'Say hello *properly*.'

It was only then that I realized. It was Amandolina.

The photos Mama sent had not prepared me for the hunched shoulders, hands stuffed into skinny jeans ripped at the knees, high-top canvas shoes smudged with dirt, and spiky short hair.

Amandolina slowly turned back to me and

103

shielded her eyes from the glare of the fluorescent lights as she stared up into my face. 'Pleased to meet you,' she said.

But she didn't look at all pleased.

3
Andi

What was everybody at school going to say when I turned up escorting the Big Friendly Giant?

I felt sick just thinking about it.

After Mum had talked to the school about Bernardo, Mrs Green had suddenly come over all friendly.

'I hear your brother from the Philippines will be joining us soon, Andi?'

'Yes, miss.' I had wondered at the chummy way she touched my shoulder, the way she looked at me, as if there was a terrible illness in the family.

'Well, if there's anything I can do to help, let me know.'

Help? I'd wondered. Why would we need help?

Now I knew.

4

Bernardo

Amandolina's eyes seemed to be fixed on my necktie and I tugged at it self-consciously.

'Very smart,' Ma said. 'Did Timbuktu make your suit?'

I nodded.

It had been a rush job. Timbuktu had refused at first. But Uncle told him it was an emergency. A cousin from out of town suddenly needed to get married. Tim understood, of course. As a tailor he often dealt with urgent weddings with fire-breathing families intent on rescuing the honour of an expectant bride. Uncle told Tim I was best man.

'Everyone on the plane will be wearing suits,' Uncle told me. 'And you must make a good first impression when you get to Heathrow.'

Tim charged extra for the rush and he charged extra for the Velcro on the tie. Tim liked Velcro. All the trousers that he'd ever made me were fastened with Velcro. The only thing about Velcro was the whole household could hear you undressing.

Zzzzt. Nardo's emptying his pockets. *Zzzzt.* Nardo's unzipped his fly.

Of course, there weren't any smart shoes to go with the suit. Nobody had ever even heard of size twenty-two in San Andres and shoes were way beyond Timbuktu's considerable abilities. So he made me a pair of leather sandals instead. Uncle said he had once seen a fashion magazine where the male models wore sandals with suits.

'Nardo, you look so smart,' Uncle had said. But I felt more like a tightly rolled piece of dim sum.

The morning of my flight to London was boiling hot long before the sun had even risen beyond the coconut trees.

Auntie made me put the jacket on, then turned me around and around as if she was inspecting a marrow for bruises.

'It's too hot, Auntie!'

'Just let me have a good look!'

I rotated, trying to ignore the rivulets of sweat that trickled down my back.

There was a knock on the door.

'Sister Sofia!' a voice called urgently from the other side.

Auntie and I looked at each other.

Whoever it was knocked again.

Auntie's shoulders sagged. She crossed the room and opened the door, leaving the chain on.

Old Tibo's face thrust through the crack, his eyes frantically searching the room behind Auntie before settling on me with relief.

'Thank God,' he said. 'I was afraid we were too late.'

'Too late for what?' Auntie's voice was cold.

'Let us in, Sister,' someone called from behind Old Tibo. 'We must speak to you.'

Auntie sighed and unlatched the chain.

A small crowd hurried into the living room.

It was so early in the morning, the streets outside should have remained empty for another hour. And yet here were all our immediate neighbours. Old Tibo, of course, with Flash Gordon at his heels. Timbuktu. Salim. Sister Len-Len with her baby curled in the crook of her elbow like a kitten.

And Jabby. He followed the others slowly into the room, frowning as he spotted the luggage piled up on the floor.

108

'It's true, then,' Old Tibo said.

Auntie glared at me.

'I swear I didn't tell anyone, Auntie!' I stared guiltily at the crowd.

'Then how did they find out?' She clenched her fists in frustration.

'I put two and two together,' Timbuktu said, his arms akimbo, a smug expression on his face. 'Your uncle wanted your jacket lined. In this climate? People only ever order suits when they're about to go on an international flight.'

'And, Nardo, there was an earthquake last night, after midnight,' Old Tibo said. 'Did you feel it?'

All their eyes turned to me, accusing.

'The first one in three years; it woke the baby,' Sister Len-Len added. Her baby made a meowing noise as if to concur. 'It's an omen.'

'Please don't send Nardo away, Sister Sofia,' Salim said. 'San Andres needs him.'

'The boy should be with his mother.' Auntie's voice was defiant, but her eyes were downcast.

'And what about us?' Old Tibo's voice quavered with anger. 'Did you think about what would happen to our barrio, our homes?'

'Superstition!' The screen door to the back banged

open as Uncle burst in. He had been getting the jeepney ready out the back. 'He's just an ordinary boy.'

'There's nothing ordinary about Bernardo,' Salim said quietly.

Everyone looked up at me.

Old Tibo shook his head. 'Brother Victor, you know the curse as well as I do. If Bernardo leaves the barrio, San Andres will be destroyed.'

I kneaded my forehead as the first pinpricks of a headache began. They were right. I was letting everyone down. San Andres needed me. 'Look, Auntie . . . Uncle,' I said softly. 'Maybe I should . . .'

'No.'

I thought at first it was Uncle who spoke because the voice was deep and dark, a man's voice. But it wasn't. It wasn't any of the grown men in the room. It was Jabby.

'Nardo, don't listen to them.' His eyes were bright.

All the mixed-up feelings of the past days welled up in me and I wanted to look away, but he held me in his laser gaze. 'You know you want to be with your mother. You must go. It's wrong for them to stop you.'

'Henry!' Sister Len-Len glared at him.

'I'm . . .' *Sorry,* I wanted to say. *I'm so sorry.*

Everyone began talking at the same time, Auntie and Uncle angry and indignant. Old Tibo and the others in furious counterpoint. Jabby saying, *No, no, no, Nardo, you must go, go, go.* The throbbing in my head turned into a deep drum-roll. I raised a hand to massage my forehead, my eyes watering. A bolt of pain slashed, lightning-sharp, into my eyes, and the faces around me whirled into a spinning blur.

And then I was conscious of a great weight.

'Nardo!' Auntie's voice was a hundred miles away.

It was in my arms again. The Earth, so wet, so heavy – and slippery despite the rough gristle of forests and mountains.

It weighed a ton. No, a million billion zillion tons. Too heavy, too heavy. I couldn't . . . It slipped and I struggled not to let go.

Then someone flicked a switch and turned off the sun.

5
Andi

Everywhere we went, eyeballs tracked Bernardo like he was an alien from outer space. But the way he behaved, you would think that *he* was the one who'd stumbled upon an alien landscape.

He hesitated at the top of the escalators for so long that a queue formed behind us. I glanced over at Mum. Didn't they have escalators in the Philippines?

But apparently he was just savouring the moment. Bernardo grinned over his shoulder. 'I cannot believe. Yesterday only, I have be in Manila.'

Mum laughed, startling a bunch of people who were coming up the escalator on the other side. 'Believe, believe!' she cried, like a mad person.

Ay kennat bileeb. His vowels were hard as stones. *His English is very good*, Ma had said the other day. Not.

I stepped past Bernardo and got on the escalator. Obviously someone had to get things moving.

Dad had taken the lift with Bernardo's trolley. He met us at the bottom of the escalator.

'All right?' he said, slapping Bernardo on the shoulder – except he missed and caught him on the elbow.

'All right.' Bernardo took a deep breath, like he was about to dive deep into the ocean. 'It have very nice smell here. Everything have air-conditioned!'

Mum thought that was funny too, braying so loudly that I'm sure I saw the airport sniffer dog check her out.

I led the way without looking over my shoulder, trying to ignore the double-takes and whispers as people caught sight of Bernardo.

'ANDI! Slow down!' Mum yelled. She handed Bernardo a ticket to feed the entry barrier but the guard opened a gate and waved him through. 'Health and safety!' he called. 'We don't want him getting stuck in them gates.'

Trolleys were not allowed on the Underground platforms so we each took one of Bernardo's suitcases to roll along. Bernardo had to bend low to reach the handle of his bag, which was just as well because he had to keep his head ducked to get through the low tunnel to the platform.

'This is first time I have train,' Bernardo said when we got to our platform. And I believed him –

especially after he leaped backwards like a terrified rabbit when the train came thundering out of the tunnel's mouth. His eyes bulged with awe as it screeched to a halt and the carriage doors rattled open.

I paused. How was he going to fit into the carriage?

But Mum was already urging him in. If the tunnels were low, the carriage was a matchbox on wheels. Bernardo practically had to unhinge his shoulders to get through the low opening. He tucked his chin deep into his chest and approached the door with his body bent into a right angle.

'Please mind the gap,' a metallic voice intoned on the PA as the carriage doors began to slide shut.

'Hurry, hurry,' Mum called, and I leaped on board as Dad swung the last bag into the carriage.

Bernardo was bent in half. It looked painful. The train set off and Mum put her arms around him, holding him up like a prop. 'Sit, Bernardo, sit!' He backed into a corner and sat on the floor, folding his knees sideways and angling his feet out into the standing space where Dad stood with the luggage. Mum stood next to him, rummaging in her handbag. She produced a thick woolly scarf. He just sat there like a baby, allowing her to wind it round his neck.

The train hissed and squealed as it rattled to the next station.

I crossed to the far end and leaned against the emergency door to the next carriage.

'Andi just needs a little time to get used to you,' Mum yelled into Bernardo's ear. I grimaced and Mum stuck her tongue out at me. She continued to yell, switching to Tagalog.

There was a loud knocking. A bunch of teenagers in the next carriage peered through the window, waving at Bernardo. He smiled and waved back and they fell about laughing. I pulled the hood of my jacket over my head.

How did Bernardo become so tall? The other Bernardo, his dad, wasn't very tall. Or was he? It was hard to tell from the portrait which now sat on the mantelpiece in our new, double-size sitting room.

As the train emerged from the tunnel, the darkness was replaced by a murky grey. Suddenly we were clacking over a high bridge, the lights of London spreading beneath the train like candles in a darkened church. There was an explosion of phones beeping and ringing all around us as the train came within reach of a mobile phone signal. Bernardo's phone went off too. OK. His message alert was Darth Vader's theme from *Star Wars*.

Mum's voice rose above the train's clatter like a foghorn. She was speaking in English again. 'Cellphones are called *mobiles* in England.'

I glanced up. Bernardo was leaning against Mum. He sat on the floor and Mum stood next to him. His head lay on her shoulder, he was that tall. He looked dead tired. He closed his eyes and rubbed his forehead with his knuckles. Mum nattered on. 'As for bananas, they say *buh-NAR-nuhs* instead of *bah-nah-nahs*. And the hood of a car is a *bonnet*. And the trunk of a car is a *boot*! A boot! Imagine!'

Bernardo nodded, smiling despite the frown that knitted his brow. He pulled his mobile from his jacket pocket. I was amazed he could manage to push the buttons with such big fingers. Mum's chatter had so obviously bored him that he was checking his messages.

I glanced at the teenagers in the next carriage. They'd forgotten about Nardo and were now pole-dancing on the other side of the carriage.

And then Mum screamed.

6
Bernardo

One moment I was surrounded by the unwelcoming committee of Old Tibo and Sister Len-Len and Salim and Tim. The next: there it was, the Earth. I actually tried to slip away before its full weight could embed itself in my shoulder, but no, no, down it went, round and heavy and wet. Instead of getting away, I bumped my head against the Tropic of Cancer and *bong!* The world made a hollow sound, like the steel water tank behind Uncle's house. Pieces of land shook off in great brown flakes and my shoulder was numbed by the cold of the polar ice cap.

I opened my eyes.

The unwelcoming committee was gone. There was just Jabby and Uncle and Auntie.

'Not again!' Auntie's voice was shrill.

'You OK, Nards?' I felt Jabby's hand on my forehead.

In fact, I felt fine. My headache was gone. I lay flat

on my back on the cool ceramic tiles of Auntie's living room.

'Sofia, cancel the flight,' Uncle said. 'Let us take him to Emergency.'

'But Old Tibo and the others will be back soon,' Jabbar said. 'They just went to get reinforcements. They'll do anything to stop Bernardo leaving.'

'Look,' Auntie said, 'Nardo is ill. He probably needs a drip or something.'

I tried to get up but Auntie's arm lay across my chest like a log. 'I feel all right now.'

The three of them looked at me. Auntie stopped leaning on my chest and I pushed myself up slowly.

'Ay,' Jabby sighed. 'Thank goodness you're back. I thought I would have to give you mouth-to-mouth resuscitation. Bet you haven't brushed your teeth this morning.'

'I have.' I smiled weakly at the joke. 'I brushed my teeth.'

'What are you feeling, Nardo? We will take you to a doctor.' Uncle's voice was urgent.

'NO!' I shook my head. 'Uh . . . really, I'm OK. I just needed something to eat. I should have listened to you, Auntie. I should have had some breakfast.

I just felt light-headed all of a sudden.' I did feel a bit light-headed so it wasn't such a lie.

Both Uncle and Auntie sank onto the sofa at the same time. They looked exhausted.

'But now I feel fine,' I said. 'Really I do.'

'Sofia.' Uncle turned to Auntie. 'Let's get him a sandwich.'

They both disappeared into the kitchen and even before the door closed they were already arguing. I could hear them through the wall. I closed my eyes. Even if they managed to agree with each other about taking me to a hospital, I was determined to leave. No way was I going to postpone my departure. If I didn't leave now, I would never do so. Old Tibo and the others would see to that.

'Nards,' Jabby said softly. 'I've got something for you. A goodbye present.'

I opened my eyes.

It was a basketball. Jabby had drawn a big smiling face on it with a thick black marker.

He handed it to me. 'And I want to say sorry. I was wrong about the team and the Giant Killers. You're right. It was not fair. So . . . this is just something to remember me by. I hope you will be happy in London.'

I didn't know what to say.

'Thanks,' I whispered.

For a moment I thought he was going to embrace me but instead he held out his hand and we shook. His eyes were suddenly red.

'Nardo!' Uncle burst into the room. 'Out the back, quick! Tibo and the others are at the door again.'

I stood up, my arms tight around the basketball.

'I'll stay here and delay them,' Jabby said. 'Go, go!'

Uncle picked up some bags and Auntie grabbed my hand and began to drag me to the back door. 'I . . . I'll email you when I get there,' I said. It sounded so inadequate. I wanted to say something more but there was nothing I could say that would change anything.

'That would be great!' Jabby forced his mouth into a grin. 'I . . . I'll see you soon.'

Which wasn't true of course.

But it was one way of saying goodbye for ever.

7
Andi

Apparently this was the third time it had happened, though we only found that out when we got home from Heathrow and Mum rang Auntie Sofia to yell at her. Apparently she and Uncle Victor had decided not to tell us about the two other seizures because they did not want us to be alarmed.

Alarming is not the word I would choose, although it ranks up there with the others. Terrifying. Horrible. Embarrassing.

When Bernardo collapsed on the tube, he slumped forward into the narrow aisle between the seats, and a sharp swerve of the train rolled him around like a giant log. He didn't even flinch. His eyes rolled to the back of his head and his body arched, his legs rigid and grotesque. Dad dived down and pulled the scarf off his neck. He ripped the tie from Bernardo's neck with a loud zip. It was attached with Velcro. But nobody laughed. Bernardo's long, long body softened for a moment and then stiffened again, like a thousand volts were shooting through him.

'Oh my God.' Mum sat, frozen in her seat, wringing her hands. 'What's wrong, Will?'

'I don't know,' Dad said. He unbuttoned Bernardo's shirt at the throat.

Bernardo had dropped his mobile on the floor. I picked it up just as it vibrated with a new text message.

Beep beep.

I stared at the tiny glowing screen.

It was a text message from the Philippines. I could tell by the +63 country code. Auntie Sofia? I pressed a key to view the message.

Another earthquake 2day. Come back.

I meant to press the red button to turn it off, but instead the phone scrolled back to the previous message.

NARDO WHY U ABANDON US?

Bernardo woke up. It took all three of us and the man sitting at the end of the carriage to sit him up in the corner again. He seemed groggy, disorientated. He collapsed against Mum, his head lolling over hers, and then suddenly he was fast asleep. We had to shake him awake when we got to our stop, and Dad had to yell down at a man on the platform to hold the train while we unloaded Bernardo and his bags.

It was only a five-minute walk to the house from the station. It felt like five hours.

'Maybe it's just jet lag,' Dad muttered softly to Mum as we guided Bernardo home. But she had her 'I'm the nurse' look on her face, pursing her lips and shaking her head. When she does that, I don't know why Dad doesn't just reply, 'Well, I'm a nurse too.'

The moment we entered the house, Mum was on the phone to Auntie Sofia. Dad, Bernardo and I stood in the hall with the luggage.

'Hello? Hello?' Mum's call had gone through. 'Can you hear me, Sofia? Can you hear me now?' Then she started yelling in Tagalog, which sounds a bit like this: *Yakataka baka yaka taka babalaba.*

It never did matter that I couldn't speak Tagalog. Mum's body language was so expressive that translating what she was probably saying had become a form of entertainment. Whenever Ma talked to Auntie Sofia, I would translate for Dad: 'She says she's glad the crocodiles are attending the disco. She says she can't wait to taste the cat food.' 'No, no, she didn't say cat food,' Dad would interrupt. 'She says the cat food was fine last time but today she'd rather dance like a chicken.'

123

Right now, she sounded really upset and whatever she was saying, it had nothing to do with dancing or chickens.

Looking at Bernardo, though, I suddenly wished that I could understand. As Mum yelled, Bernardo kept his eyes on the floor, his body getting more and more hunched until it was as if his head had disappeared between his bony shoulders.

Mum suddenly appeared at the door, the phone still pressed to her ear, her eyes staring and frantic. *'William, it's happened twice already! TWICE!'*

'Make yourself at home,' Dad said to Bernardo quietly. He followed Mum into the living room.

Bernardo straightened, the ceiling light behind him gently bumping against the back of his head. His eyes were totally red.

'I am the blame,' he said softly. 'I am the blame.' He rubbed his eyes. Oh God, he was crying. What was I supposed to do? Should I put my arms around him? I took a tiny step forward.

. Dad reappeared at the living-room door. 'Well,' he said, the fake cheerfulness in his voice matching the fake smile on his face. 'While Mum's *chatting* on the phone, why don't you show Bernardo to your room, Andi? He might want to freshen up. Take a shower.'

How could Dad act like nothing was going on? I glared at him but he was looking way above my head at Bernardo.

'Take him up, Andi.' There was a sharp edge to Dad's voice. 'Now.'

I turned and led the way to the stairs. At the bottom of the staircase, I stepped back and said, 'You first.'

He flashed a wan smile over his shoulder. '*Salamat*. Thank you.'

Following behind him was terrifying. It was like walking behind a very tall tree. He teetered with every step, as if any minute he was going to lose his balance and come crashing down on me. But we survived, and at the top he smiled encouragingly at me.

'In there,' I said, pointing at the door with the Toxic Twins poster Blu-Tacked to it.

Bernardo bent down to step through my doorway and immediately toppled over. Oh God. Was he having another fit?

But he'd only tripped over my basketball, which he didn't see because he was so tall. Or maybe he didn't see it because it was so dark.

I turned on the light.

Bernardo had landed on the mattresses Mum had laid out on the floor. He rolled over on his back and gazed around him, mouth wide open.

What was he staring at? Did I leave a pair of knickers on the floor?

'What is it?' I muttered crossly.

Bernardo pointed at Michael Jordan dribbling a ball above my bedstead, and then at Michael Jordan dunking a ball in a hoop, then Michael Jordan flying in the air with his Air Jordans akimbo, then Michael Jordan posing with Bugs Bunny in that cartoon.

'What, what?' I said, impatient.

'Michael Jordan,' Bernardo said, grinning like an idiot. 'Michael Jordan is my biggest fan.'

8
Bernardo

'**H**ere you go, sweetie.' The technician's English was soft and elegant like a character from an old black and white movie. She was beautiful. Her hair was black, a dark frame to the symmetry of her face. Her sparkly, pale pink lipstick was a perfect match for her coffee skin. Her lashes were extravagant, rimming her eyes like an Egyptian princess. *S. Patel*, the badge on her jacket lapel said.

'What your name?' I murmured.

She smiled. 'My name is Sunita. And it says here your name is Bernard, is that right?'

I nodded. She asked so kindly, I didn't feel like correcting her. Anyway, 'Bernard' sounded English.

'How old are you, Bernard?'

'Sixteen.'

Sunita laughed a tinkly sort of laugh. 'You are a tall lad, aren't you?'

Tall lad.

The way she put it sounded so nice. Like something to be proud of.

I nodded as I gazed deep into the dark pools of her eyes.

It was a machine for imaging the brain, Ma had said. Its invisible rays drilled deep, searching for answers to questions that had not yet been asked.

'Down you go, Bernard.' Sunita helped me lie down on the patient table, supporting my neck with a downy arm. My legs dangled down at the knees: the table was too short. Her fingers were like butterflies as she stroked the hair away from my eyes.

She placed a rolled-up towel on either side of my head. 'This will help you keep still,' she said. She covered me with a blue cotton blanket. 'And this will make you feel more comfortable.' She fitted a pair of earphones playing pop music over my ears. 'These are for the noise.'

Sunita took what looked like a waste-paper basket cut lengthwise and fitted it over my face. And then she pressed a button and the table levitated up to the machine's mouth.

'There is a lot of noise, but don't worry, you won't feel a thing.' Her voice sounded far away. 'Some people feel a bit funny in the machine and I don't blame them. There's a button inside. If you really can't stand it any more, just press the button and I'll take you out.' She leaned up close. 'Think of it as having your picture taken. Only noisier. And longer. The whole session will take about thirty minutes. Close your eyes, sweetie. Think happy thoughts.'

She left and I closed my eyes. When was the last time I'd slept properly? The plane crew had upgraded me to Business Class, where there was more room, but the seats were only inches better. And that teeny tiny toilet! It had been a long flight – and not just because it took fourteen hours.

'Ready now, Bernard?' Miss Patel's voice seemed a long way away.

'Ready.'

The machine began to scream, completely drowning out Tom Jones.

Then the table began to move and slowly I was swallowed by the tube. This was what it was like to be buried alive.

And all the time, the machine screamed.

I wanted to press my hands against my ears but I could not move my arms. I wanted to cry out but nobody was going to hear me above that noise. The tube screamed and groaned and banged.

'Think happy thoughts,' Miss Patel had said.

I tried.

I thought of Michael Jordan and Amandolina and basketball.

Of Auntie and Mama and Uncle William.

Of being in England at last.

But the thoughts drifted away like smoke.

Think happy thoughts.

I decided to think of the lovely Sunita, conjuring the beautiful face framed in the long dark hair.

But it was not Sunita's face that took shape before me. The face that emerged from my swirling thoughts was beautiful, yes, but there was a sulkiness in the dark eyes and disdain in the turn of the lips.

It was Gabriela.

The lips parted to show white teeth. But the voice when it came was that of Mad Nena.

Nardo, she whispered. *The earthquakes have begun.*

9
Andi

So after Bernardo informed me that Michael Jordan was his biggest fan, Mum suddenly burst into the room yelling that Bernardo had to go to A&E.

I was in the middle of figuring out how to tell him he'd got it the wrong way round. *Bernardo* was *Michael Jordan's* biggest fan, surely. Unless, of course, there was something else about my half-brother that Mum had not told me.

But before I could say anything, Mum was marching him down the stairs. Bernardo didn't even get the chance to change out of his travelling clothes except to ditch the shiny jacket.

'You're cold,' Mum said, as if Bernardo couldn't figure it out himself. I looked at him and was surprised to realize, yeah, he was cold. In fact, there was a tinge of purple under his lips, like someone who'd been swimming at an open-air lido.

Mum made him wear Dad's long fur-lined coat,

which was the colour of poo, a knitted cap, also the colour of poo, and a scarf. Strangely, the coat seemed too big and broad for his narrow frame, though the arms came to just above his wrists. He looked a right wally but he didn't complain. If it was me, Mum would have had a fight on her hands. But Bernardo obviously wasn't anything like me.

It was after midnight when they left. I was insanely curious about what was wrong with Bernardo but Mum wouldn't let me come along. She said I had to go to bed because I had school the next day. She made Dad go to bed too because he had an early shift at the hospital.

When I was really little, Mum used to say, 'If you go on being naughty like that, I'll take you to A&E.' And I used to stop whatever I was doing and sit down on the floor, my hands folded on my lap, demure as anything.

That ended when I turned seven and knew better. I mean, Mum is an A&E nurse. She went there every day. Which made *her* and all the A&E doctors and nurses the naughtiest people in the world.

Right now, they were probably giving Bernardo an enema or draining his blood or tapping him for spinal fluid or shaving his head or sucking out his brain.

That's what they do at A&E.

The phone woke me at two in the morning. It rang and rang but Dad wasn't picking up. I could hear him snoring across the hall. I went downstairs and answered it. It was Mum, of course.

'I just wanted you to know that everything is fine: they're giving Nardo an MRI right now.'

'What's that?'

'MRI? Magnetic Resonance Imaging. They're scanning his brain.'

I knew it! They always went for the brain. 'For what?'

'Can I speak to Dad?'

'He's asleep.' After all that fuss about Dad needing his sleep – it was just like Mum to want to wake him up now because she felt like sharing. 'Mum, why does Bernardo need a brain scan?'

She ignored me. 'Get Dad.'

The other day I spotted a piece in a magazine about Neutralizing Flashpoints. I only read it because I thought it was a new film at the cinema.

But it turned out that Flashpoints referred to good old-fashioned family rows. And Neutralizing was just fancy jargon for telling everyone to stay cool. The secret? Information. Apparently parents could

Neutralize Flashpoints by simply keeping their teenagers *informed* about what was going on.

Mum would get an F in Neutralizing Flashpoints.

I ran up the stairs and shook Dad awake. He shambled down to the telephone without even opening his eyes. He didn't have to say much. He just grunted while Mum talked and talked. Then he put the phone down and was on his way up before I managed to say, 'Dad, what did Mum say?'

But he had already disappeared into the bedroom.

Neutralizing Flashpoints – haven't you heard of it, Dad?

10
Bernardo

The earphones were meant to block out the MRI's noise but I could still hear everything. The banging and crashing and the electronic whining.

And Gabriela.

Nardo, she whispered. The voice was not Gabriela's. It was Mad Nena's. *You left.*

'Leave me alone,' I said through clenched teeth.

You left, she laughed. *And now it's going to be all your fault.*

Then I remembered the button. Sunita said if I pressed the button, she would stop the machine and get me out. But what would I tell her? How could I tell her about Gabriela?

I closed my eyes and tried not to listen to the machine's screaming.

When I first met Gabriela, I was only thirteen.

It was the same year Ma's famous letter arrived, just a week after my thirteenth birthday:

They told me your visa should be ready in a few days so you must start getting ready. You will be on a plane to London in just two weeks!

After we read the letter, Uncle, Auntie and I were so happy we jumped up and down for a long time.

I remember thinking it was the best birthday present ever! At long last, I was going to London!

My head was full of plans. I would bring the catapult Uncle had made me out of mango wood. I would ask Jabby to lend me the woolly jumper that a relative had sent him from America. It was too hot to wear in San Andres anyway.

And presents. I couldn't go to London without presents for Ma and Uncle Will and Amandolina.

I had been saving my centavos in a piggy bank shaped like a London bus that Ma had sent long ago. I emptied the coins on the floor and counted them. I would use half of the money to buy a box of sweet pili nut *turrones* for Mama and Uncle William. And the other half? I was going to buy puka shells from Sister Len-Len, to string into a necklace for dear little Amandolina.

Amandolina would have been ten. I liked to imagine that she would be like Jabby's younger sister, Pet, who was about the same age.

Pet was always needing Jabby to walk her to school or braid her hair or tell her a story. Pet the Pain, he called her. When she rushed to hug him after school, he always wrinkled his nose and muttered, 'Pet? She's more like a pest.' But I could tell he liked it. *I* would.

That morning on my way to school, I stopped at Sister Len-Len's roadside stall, where she sold seashells to tourists on their way to the beach. The puka shells were more expensive than I had remembered but Sister Len-Len kindly measured out an extra portion, just because it was for my little sister.

Jabby had a new basketball with him but I cried off a game at recess because I wanted to work on Amandolina's necklace. When the bell rang, I rushed out to the frangipani tree in the back playground where I knew I would not be disturbed.

But I had not reckoned on Gabriela and her gang. By some unlucky twist, they had decided to sit under the frangipani tree instead of on their usual bench.

I knew Gabriela by then. I no longer needed Jabby to warn me away from her. I could see what she and her gang of girl thugs did to the other children.

By the time I realized that they were there, it was too late.

They did not give me a chance to run away. Three

of the girl thugs grabbed me and manhandled me to the spot behind the tree where Gabriela was waiting. She looked pleased, like a cat that had just been dangled a juicy mouse.

'You're that little boy with the giant's name!' Gabriela reached out and stroked my hair. I struggled to get away but Gabriela's girlfriends were stronger and bigger than me. Then I thought, Why not just co-operate, get it over with? What could Gabriela do to me? I had no money. I was worth nothing to her.

'What giant's name?' one of her thugs asked.

'Bernardo.' Gabriela's eyes glittered like the dew on the frangipani's broad leaves. 'His name is Bernardo. Like Bernardo Carpio.'

The girls laughed and shook me hard like they were shaking fruit from a tree.

'So. Bernardo. What have you got?' one said. But instead of waiting for me to reply, they swung me up and over like a floppy rag doll, dangling me upside down so that the few coins I had left fell out of my pockets. And then, to my dismay, the small brown paper package with shells for Amandolina's necklace tumbled out.

'Jackpot!' Gabriela laughed as she snatched up the package.

A helpless fury suddenly filled me. 'NO!' I shouted. 'That's for my sister! Leave it alone!'

But shouting was pointless. I knew that nobody in the playground was going to come to my rescue. Not the children. Not the teachers. Gabriela's thugs pushed me down on the ground, hard. I fell awkwardly, banging my head and shoulder on the hard earth.

'Ah, puka shells!' Gabriela smirked at me. 'What a lovely brother. Were you making a necklace for your sister?'

I didn't answer, watching with disbelief as she examined the shells.

'I like necklaces. Remember this?' She pulled the wishing stone from her collar. 'My mama made this for me.'

I leaped up, throwing myself on her. She flinched as my fingernails grazed her arm. 'Stupid boy!' She slapped me hard on the face with her other hand.

Her thugs peeled me off and shoved me down on the ground, kicking and punching until I could only curl up in a ball, my arms over my head.

'Don't you know the rules of Sacred Heart Academy, Bernardo?' Gabriela nudged me with the toe of her foot. 'Rule One: Gabriela is always right. And what is Rule Two, girls?'

Her thugs replied in chorus: 'Rule Two: Refer to Rule One!'

They laughed as they walked away, my precious package clutched in Gabriela's hand.

I uncurled and lay flat on my back staring up at the spreading branches of the frangipani tree, the tears streaming down my face. I had no money left to get Amandolina anything else. She was going to be so disappointed. I grabbed a handful of my hair and pulled as hard as I could but the pain could not distract me from my failure.

I wished I had not chosen to sit under the frangipani tree.

I wished I had waited until after school to buy the shells.

I wished that my immigration papers had not come through so that this would never have happened.

And then, of course, it turned out that the immigration papers weren't coming after all.

Ma wrote to say sorry, the Home Office wanted more paperwork, whatever that meant.

11
Andi

Truth to tell, I had always regarded Bernardo as a partner waiting to happen. He's a boy, isn't he? He and I were going to go running, play basketball, do sport.

And I could tell Bernardo would have been willing. He loved Michael Jordan. I loved Michael Jordan.

But no. That body. Even if he wanted to, he just couldn't. And of course it was not his fault. *I am the blame.*

No, no. He was not the blame, poor guy. Just unlucky.

He's not the blame that I am so totally disappointed.

I was already dressed in my school uniform, pouring some Coco Pops into a bowl, when they finally returned from the hospital.

Dad had already left for his double shift.

Bernardo looked ghastly. He seemed to teeter even

141

more as he stood there, looking down at the breakfast table, so tall his head was in the shadows above the table's pendant light. Mum's hair stood on end like she'd just crawled through a bush. Neither of them smelled sweet and I moved upwind of the table to finish my Coco Pops.

She poured Bernardo a bowl of cereal even though his eyelids were sliding down over his eyes every few minutes. He sat down and the chair bowed visibly.

'So what happened?' I said. 'What did they say?'

'We won't know until Doctor Grant has had a look at the scans. They sent us home.'

'You were there all night and they didn't tell you anything?'

Mum made a face at me.

There was a soft clunk and we realized that Bernardo had fallen asleep, his head cradled on one arm, his spoon in his hair.

Mum clicked her tongue the way she does and gently shook him awake. She escorted him up the stairs to my room. When she came down again fifteen minutes later, she was dressed in her nurse's uniform, her hair swept back in a professional bun. But her eyes were red-rimmed with exhaustion.

'You've got nothing on after school, have you,

Andi?' Mum said. 'What time do you get home today?'

'Why?' I looked at her through veiled lids. She had a guilty expression on her face. This was not a motherly enquiry into my wellbeing.

Mum sighed. 'Look, I booked the day off but one of the other nurses is sick.'

'You're going to work?'

'I'll be back after eight tonight. Dad is on that double shift. He won't be in until after bedtime.'

'Mum, how can you do that? You had so much time to plan for Bernardo's first day!'

'I know, but it can't be helped.'

I could feel my chest tightening. This didn't sound good.

'Anyway, I want you to look out for Bernardo when you get home.'

'What?' How was I supposed to look after a sixteen-year-old?

'Please, Andi. Just keep him company. He doesn't know where anything is. He's never been outside San Andres. Look, if you don't want to look after him, *help* him. Just help him, Andi.'

'But, Mum—'

'He'll still be jetlagged. He will probably sleep all

day. I've marinated some chicken in the fridge. Forty-five minutes in a medium oven . . .'

'MUM!' I was supposed to babysit him AND feed him? This was worse than getting a pet.

But Mum was already on her way out, adjusting the little nametag that she wore at the hospital.

'Thank you, darling, I really appreciate it.'

12
Bernardo

It had been morning when my plane took off from Manila. And it was still the same day when I landed in London, even though I'd been travelling for sixteen hours and, back in Manila, the date had changed.

It was not an exaggeration to say that I had travelled backwards in time.

So? I could imagine Jabby joking about it. *You arrived several hours YOUNGER. You have nothing to complain about.*

No, but the time-travelling left me . . . unbalanced. And last night's rush to hospital did not help.

When the doctors had finished pricking and prodding and weighing and measuring and testing, Mama took me home.

I was so tired I don't remember much about bedtime except Mama hugging me as I sat on the mattress on the floor. A thought briefly crossed my mind that this was a momentous occasion, my first bedtime in London. But I was so tired, too tired. She stroked my forehead like a baby, then tucked the quilt high under my chin. It pulled right off my feet. 'Oh, Bernardo,' Ma sighed. She left and returned with another quilt to cover my legs.

'Amandolina will be here when you wake up,' she whispered as she turned to go. 'I'll see you after work this evening, darling Nardo.'

And then Ma drew the curtains shut and I tumbled down, down, down into the utter darkness of a bottomless pit.

13
Andi

Lunch time. I avoided the playground and went into the new gym, ignoring the sign that said *No Entry Unless Authorized*.

Avoiding Rocky had become an integral part of my daily school routine:

Enter by the side gate in case Rocky and his friends were hanging out in front of Saint Simeon's.

Stay in the library until the bell went.

Eat my packed lunch in a secluded corner, then head straight for the new gym to shoot hoops until the bell rang for afternoon lessons.

I could forget all my troubles when I played. Goodness knows I deserved some upside after finding out I had Fee-fi-fo-fum for a big brother.

It was not as bad as it sounded. Saint Simeon's gymnasium was fantastic: it even had three-point lines painted on – at my previous school, we didn't have three-point lines so all my cool long-distance shots were wasted.

Lucky for me, the ball lockers were fastened with the same crummy locks as my old school. It took only one elbow and a kick for the door to fall open. I extracted a basketball and pushed through the double doors to the court.

Oh Holy Mother of God.

There was someone else there, shooting baskets. Someone so tall and hench, he was virtually bursting out of his shirt.

Rocky.

He took aim at the basket and released the ball. He missed.

I whirled round to leave but Rocky's ball beat me to the exit and banged hard on the double doors in front of me.

'Hey!'

Oh Holy Mother of God, he spotted me.

I turned round and faked a smile. 'Hi.'

He looked like he wanted to laugh. 'You look different in school uniform.'

And you look as stupid in your tie as I do in my skirt, I thought. But what I said aloud was: 'So do you.'

'Your name is Andi, right?'

'Andi with an *i*.' I turned towards the door. 'Well, gotta go.'

'Wait!' Rocky called. 'Were you going to shoot some hoops?'

No, I was going to plant some rice. 'I was just going to pass the time.'

'One on one?'

I don't know what got into me. Instead of marching out of the court, I spun round and passed him my ball. He caught it, leaping into the air like Kareem Abdul-Jabbar on hydraulics to hook it at the goal. It looped over our heads but bounced harmlessly off the back board.

I raced after it. Rocky didn't bother to run after me, he just positioned himself under the basket waiting to pounce when I came close for the shot. No chance, mister. I stopped at the three-point line and made my shot. *Swish*. The look on his face was a prize.

'Pow!' He punched the air, staring at me in wonder. 'Hey, Andi, you didn't say you were good.'

You didn't ask, I thought. But pleasure spread through my stomach like warm water. I shrugged, my face expressionless as I went to collect the ball from under the basket. I toed the three-point line and took another shot. *Swish*.

Rocky shook his head in wonder and grabbed the ball. 'Show me some more.'

We played for the rest of the break. Rocky sank exactly two shots. I didn't count how many baskets I made. I just stayed away from him, running wide – no point getting up close with Rocky blocking the way like a plaster. I shot from the three-point line. *Swish. Swish. Swish.*

After fifteen solid minutes, we stopped to drink from the water fountain beside the court. My cotton blouse stuck to my back, wet with sweat. But I felt good.

'You don't miss, do you?'

'Nope.'

'You're amazing. You're exactly what the Souls need.'

I stared hopefully up at him. But the doleful expression on his face was enough. He didn't mean it.

'I'm sorry, Andi. I can't change the rules.'

The bell rang. I tossed Rocky the ball and turned away, avoiding the searching look in his eyes. 'Thanks for the workout.'

Before I could push through the double doors of the exit, Rocky yelled, 'Wait!'

He sprinted up to me, tossing the ball. I caught it instinctively.

'There's nothing in the rulebook that says you can't train with us.' The brown eyes glowed warmly down at me and the quick rush of blood to my cheeks almost distracted me from what he was saying. 'Wanna come? You'll have some fun and you could definitely teach the boys a thing or two.'

'You mean it?'

'Sure.' Rocky waved as he disappeared out of the door. 'Sunday afternoon. Two p.m. at the outdoor courts near the hospital. Be there!'

As the double doors at the other end of the court flapped shut behind him, I stood there like an idiot. Then the meaning of what Rocky had said penetrated my brain.

YES! I jumped high, releasing the ball as I leaped. It flew true and swished into the basket without touching the sides of the metal ring.

Suddenly I had a chance. Training with the Souls was just a few steps away from becoming one of the team.

'Andi!'

I whirled round. Mrs Green? How did she beam herself into the gym without my noticing?

'You know that playing in the gym during break is forbidden.'

'I uh . . .'

'See me in detention. After school.'

14
Bernardo

It was dark when I woke.

I got up slowly from the mattress on Amandolina's bedroom floor and drew the curtains. Nothing. The room remained dark. I could see a street lamp glowing outside. I flicked on the light switch by the door and immediately spotted the note taped to the knob.

> Bernardo, I will be back from school
> @ 4 p.m. U R not allowed to do
> ANYTHING until I get back.

It was signed with a massive letter 'A' – for Amandolina, I suppose, except the A had a pair of horns.

Back at 4 p.m.? The digital clock on Amandolina's bedside table said 5:00 – five what? Could it be 5 a.m. in the morning? But that would be silly, wouldn't it? If it were morning, Amandolina would be in her bed next to mine and the roosters would be crowing. But wait, this was London. There were no roosters. Most likely it was 5 p.m. and Amandolina was either late coming home from school or downstairs in the kitchen.

'Amandolina?' I stood at the top of the stairs and listened. But the silence from downstairs was deafening. There was definitely nobody at home.

I shivered, suddenly aware of the cold gnawing on my bare feet, neck and arms.

I looked down at myself. I was in the same shirt and trousers I was wearing when I got off the plane. I smelled like onions left out on the chopping board.

I had to wash.

I went to the bathroom.

There was a real bathtub.

San Andres was a village known for what it didn't have and a bath was definitely on that list. A shower served its purpose. Or a tall bucket of water and a *tabo*, a plastic beaker to ladle water on yourself.

I stared at the bathtub – not that I'd never seen one before; I've seen them plenty of times in American movies – but how was I going to sit inside it? I could not possibly fold myself small enough and neat enough to fit. Besides, the thought of immersing myself in water infused with the dirt and odours I was trying to get rid of was nauseating.

What would Jabby say? *Get a grip, Bernardo! Use your coconut!*

I decided to fill the tub with water and *kneel* next to it and wash myself as per usual – a saucepan from the kitchen would make as good a *tabo* as any. I found the rubber stopper and plugged the hole.

But then the tap marked H for hot ran cold. And the tap marked C for cold ran freezing.

I left both taps running and hurried downstairs to the kitchen. The electric kettle on the counter was far too small for the quantity of hot water I needed. I searched the cupboards and took out the biggest pot I could find, filling it with water, then putting it on the stove to heat. I could mix the heated water with the cold in the tub for a warm bath. Problem solved.

I went up to Amandolina's room and found my suitcase behind the door. I needed a change of clothes. I unzipped the bag and pulled out a fresh pair of trousers and a T-shirt. Something solid dropped out onto the floor. My heart leaped.

Gabriela's stone.

*   *   *

Do you feel guilty, Giant Boy? Guilty about Gabriela? Guilty for what you did to me?

Mad Nena.

Always sneaking along behind me. Staring from behind lampposts. Waiting outside the school gates. Praying. Mumbling. Now that I'd finally put a whole world between me and her, I was glad that she wasn't going to be bothering me any more.

Do you feel guilty? Guilty? Guilty?

Not guilty. I didn't deserve her accusations despite what happened. I didn't even know that Nena was Gabriela's mother. Although I should have guessed. There was a similarity in the arch of their eyebrows, the curl of their lips. Gabriela was a young beauty and Nena was – used to be – a handsome woman.

She was the village witch.

And she terrorized San Andres in the same way Gabriela terrorized the school.

She wielded good magic and bad. White magic – love potions and spells for fine weather and high grades – was not her bread and butter, though she rarely turned away business when it came.

Black magic was her big ticket, the ruin of a rice crop, a plague of dengue fever, the seduction of a virgin, the nasty accident. Her clientele came from far away and crossed her palm with the kind of wealth people in San Andres could only dream of.

Who would dare defy that kind of power? Who would dare stand up to a woman like Nena?

She and Gabriela had a dog named Judas, a cross between a German shepherd and a boxer. Nena once turned up with Judas on our street and Old Tibo's dog, Flash Gordon, rushed joyfully towards him to sniff his bottom as friendly dogs do. Flash Gordon would do anything for a pat on the head. But Judas, it turned out, was not of the same love-hungry mould. Judas was vicious for no other reason than that he was born vicious. Poor Flash Gordon found that out soon enough – and now has half an ear to show for it.

Shopkeepers looked the other way when Nena bypassed the till or helped herself to an extra measure of rice or grabbed another tin of tuna. Far better for the books to fall short than to suffer some mysterious illness.

Tricycle cabs stopped for her even when they had passengers. The passengers got off without complaint and let her have their fare. It was said that she was quick to punish any sign of disrespect.

Sebastian, the tricycle driver, was in such a rush to meet his girlfriend one day that he didn't stop when

Nena tried to flag his cab. People nearby saw Nena raise one crimson-nailed finger in a strange gesture. One of the tyres on Sebastian's tricycle blew out with a massive bang. He careened into a bus speeding in the opposite direction.

He didn't stand a chance.

At school, Gabriela exacted from us the same obedience and terror that her witch mother commanded from our parents. Gabriela and her gang ran roughshod over the playground on a daily basis. They got away with everything. My little packet of shells was only one small item in a long list of delinquencies.

So maybe I was being foolish when I decided to do what I did. Or maybe it was because I was just thirteen and had no sense. Or maybe the news that I wasn't going to London after all made me reckless.

I don't know.

Maybe I was just being totally, utterly stupid.

I decided to pay Gabriela back. I would steal that necklace she was always dangling at me. Then she would know how it felt to lose something.

But what happened next was not of my making.

Guilty.

Mad Nena's voice whispered in my ears like poison.

No, I'm not.

Coward. Running away.

'I am NOT running away,' I said aloud.

Loser!

'Leave me alone.' I covered my ears.

It's boiled itself dry!

'Boiled itself . . .?' I started at the illogical words.

'THE POT!' It was not Gabriela – it was Amandolina, screaming frantically at the bedroom door.

'IT'S BOILED ITSELF DRY! AND THE BATH! YOU LEFT IT RUNNING AND IT'S FLOODED EVERYTHING!'

15
Andi

Surprise, surprise, it was all my fault.

'If you had come home at four like you promised, this would not have happened!' Mum yelled.

'I was in detention!' I yelled back.

'Detention! Of all days to behave badly!'

'I wasn't behaving badly!'

'But you were in detention!'

'I left Bernardo a *note*. I told him not to do ANYTHING!'

'But you were *LATE*!'

And on and on and on.

Anyway, the upshot was: Mum grounded me for a week.

Which, of course, was convenient. Now Bernardo was guaranteed his babysitter after school every day and Mum and Dad could do all the double shifts they wanted at the hospital. Mum couldn't have planned it better.

How was I to know that Bernardo would try to run a bath? A DINGBAT from the MOON would've known to watch the boiling pot and mind the running bath. It's not like being FOREIGN exempts you from COMMON SENSE.

I mean, he's sixteen. He's practically an adult. I'm just thirteen. I'm barely a teenager.

He left Mum's best soup pot burning on the stove. It was ruined. The carpet in the hall was ruined. The ceiling under the bathroom crumbled to pieces. Ruined.

I was the one who raised the alarm. *I* was the one who turned off the heat. *I* turned off the taps. *I* cleared up the mess. Well. Bernardo spent hours scraping that pot with a scourer, but that was nothing. I mopped up the bathroom and covered the carpet with towels. But nobody's going to thank me for that, are they?

'Thank you, Amandolina,' Bernardo whispered.

OK. Now Bernardo was making me feel guilty. I sneaked a glance at him. He sat on his mattress with his back to my bed and his knees drawn up to his chin and both hands clasped over his knees.

'What for?'

'I am the blame.'

YES, YOU ARE THE BLAME! You are the reason I've got half a bedroom and now I've got half a life as well. You are the blame the blame the BLAME!

'Nah.' I flopped down on the mattress, scowling at my socks. 'It wasn't your fault. You don't know anything.'

'I don't know anything,' Bernardo repeated like he needed to memorize it. 'I don't know anything.'

Oh shut up. But aloud I said, 'It wasn't your fault.'

Bernardo grabbed my hand. I was so surprised I tried to snatch it back.

He smiled at me and gently put something on my palm.

'What's this, Bernardo?' It was a smooth flat black stone, the kind that's perfect for skipping on the ocean. There was a hole bored into it where a chain could slip through.

'It have magic,' he was whispering now. I had to bend my head close to his to hear what he was saying. 'You make wish. Wish come true.'

What was I supposed to say to that? Should I tell him now that I don't believe in magic and have never even read Harry Potter? Should I tell him that I do not bother to read the fortune cookies that come with the Chinese takeaway?

This was what I said: 'Really? Is that so?'

Bernardo swivelled round so that he was leaning on one elbow, looking squarely into my eyes. He was close enough for me to see the pupils blooming to the edges of his amber irises.

He took the stone from my hand and clasped it against his chest like he was about to pledge his loyalty to the Queen. 'I have sorry about the flooding, Amandolina,' he said softly. 'Please. Make a wish. Don't say loud. Just wish with your head.'

16

Bernardo

From: Mary Ann Hipolito-Jones
            mahjones@gmail.com
To: Hipolito, Sofia
Subject: From Bernardo

Dear Auntie and Uncle,

Kumusta? How are you? How have you been up to?

Mama borrowed me her email so that I could make news to you about life here in London. I write you in English because I must practise before I have school on Monday. It's up for me to be fitted in.

Mama, Uncle William and Amandolina are making their best so I feel like home. Uncle William always says he loves to have me. He is good.

It have very cold in England but inside the house it have very warm because the house makes heating. Now and there I really miss you, especially when the house makes cold.

I have some mistake at the beginning but Mama

164

teach me how to use bathtub now. I just have to take things slow by slow.

Yesterday was Saturday and Mama took me shopping for clothes. We went to internet shop TallMan.com – there have a house where they keep stock of shoes, clothes, everything for Tall Man – like me!

Mama buy me very nice rubber shoes – in London rubber shoes are called trainers. Imagine me now I have rubber shoes! I cannot believe. The trainers so comfort, they have shock-absorbing soles and breathable fabric according to the box. I have happiness so much. So many years I wear rubber slippers or sandals because no shoes fitting me. Timbuktu sandals good but London very too cold to have bare toes.

Mama also buy me four T-shirt, four pair sock, two pair jean (tell Timbuktu I have wear the trousers he made me on special occasion only), pyjamas, two sweater, one fleece hoodie very warm, one tracksuit very warm. Uncle William's jacket fit me so we have no need to buy coat. Anyway, Uncle William's jacket is as brand as new.

I miss you. Please give my regards to Jabby, Sister Len-Len, Salim and Old Tibo.

Love,

Nardo

PS Don't worry about happened in train. I am OK now. I have brain scan.

From: Jabbar theoneandonly@hotmail.com
To: Hipolito-Jones, Mary Ann
Subject: Pls pass to Nardo 'Michael Jordan' Hipolito

Dir Nardo,

Sister Sofia show me your email n I was very impress!!!!!!!! You R now d genuine English gentleman speaking d Queen English like James Bond dressed in d genuine English hoodie. D brain scan sound like gud idea – maybe dey find your brain at last!!!!!!!!

Bad news about Mountain Men. D new contractor said more building work needed. What a waste of a good basketball court! Not yet ready for grand opening. So our game wid Giant Killers postponed until further notice. Bad trip, man.

But never mind. My secret entrance still there. So I go every day to d Arena to shoot hoops.

Without further adieu,

Jabs

17
Andi

Like Cinderella I closed my eyes and wished.
I even had a little debate in my head: wish for
something that could actually happen, wish it won't
rain tomorrow . . . or wish for something noble like
Peace on Earth for ever and ever amen. But no. I
wished for the impossible. I wished that the Souls
would make me their point guard.

Which would have been grand if I actually did
believe in magic stones.

Of course I don't so it didn't matter what I wished.

It was worth it, though, if only to see the smile on
Bernardo's face – so wide I thought his head would
split in half.

Dad and I were watching TV when they got back
from the Tall Man shop. Ma said she found the shop
on the internet and the blurb had said 'for men six
foot four and taller'.

Bernardo was already wearing his new clothes. He

167

looked so pleased – you would have thought he'd won the lottery.

The Tall Man shop should have called itself the Old Man shop – the T-shirts had collars, the trousers were high-waisted with turn-ups, the trainers were boring white, no stripes, no brand, no nothing – but anything was better than those horrible home-made sandals and Velcro trousers. I don't suppose Tall Man had much of a range – there can't be that many Shrek-size men in England.

Apparently trousers were hemmed on the shop floor to make sure they fitted even the tallest people. Who would have thought there was such a place?

In fact, Bernardo looked OK.

More than OK.

He looked almost normal.

He looked warm too (Mum bought him two sweaters and he had *both* on, and the fleece, and the tracksuit jacket, and we were *indoors*). Which made me realize how cold he must have been since he arrived.

No wonder he boiled the house.

'TA-DAA!' Mum said with a theatrical flourish.

Bernardo bowed from the waist, his head just missing the pendant lamp in the sitting room.

Dad had a hand over his mouth like he was stifling a cry of joy. Then he got up and hugged Bernardo (around the chest, by the way, because unless Bernardo walked around on his knees it was impossible to reach anywhere near the top of his head) and said, 'You look terrific, son.'

Huh. I could tell it was only a matter of time before Dad was going to tell Bernardo to call him Dad.

'Call me Dad,' Dad said, and his eyes were kind of red and puffy like he felt like crying. Mum's eyes got red and puffy too and they leaned towards each other like two old trees.

My eyes stung and I rubbed them. Crowd hysteria. One person starts crying and it sets everyone off. I opened my eyes and realized that Mum was glaring at me. She obviously thought it was my turn to say something nice or at least burst into tears.

So I said, 'Yeah, Bernardo. You look really cool.' I meant it too. Cool. As in: no longer *un*cool.

'Thanks you,' Bernardo said.

'You are welcomes,' I said and Mum scowled at me. As if Bernardo was the type to get upset about a little joke.

But truly, I was glad for Bernardo. The guy deserved a break.

An hour later, I was sitting on my bed, reading *Lay-up Magazine,* when Mum came into our room with a bin bag which she began to fill with all the Velcro clothes he'd brought from the Philippines. Bernardo burst in after her. It was the first time I'd seen him . . . angry.

'Ma! *NO!*'

'Nardo, you won't be wearing these any more!' Mum held up the Velcro tie, wrinkled her nose and stuffed it into the bag.

Bernardo snatched the tie from the bag and threw it back into the wardrobe.

I couldn't believe it. Bernardo *didn't* want to get rid of his horrible old clothes. He actually thought they were cool.

'Mama, Timbuktu made them for me, special quality!'

'Ay, that Timbuktu. That tailor is the reason why the whole of San Andres is a fashion disaster zone!'

'But, Mama!'

'Nardo, when you go to school on Monday and meet the other kids, you will thank me.'

For once, I agreed with Mum. But in the end she had to compromise, allowing Bernardo to keep the Velcro suit he arrived in. There's no accounting for taste. Hopefully there will be no opportunities for him to wear it ever again.

Mum made large eyes at me as Bernardo sat on the floor, folding away his new clothes. She gave a slight tilt of her head. She wanted me to follow her downstairs.

In the kitchen, she gestured for me to sit down.

'I just want to explain about Bernardo, Andi,' she said in a low voice. 'I haven't told him but his scan has come back.'

'Why haven't you told him?'

Mum didn't answer that one, she just kept talking. 'Bernardo has a tumour in his pituitary gland. That's the bit right at the root of his brain. The tumour has been producing abnormal amounts of growth hormone, that's why Bernardo is so . . . tall. If Sofia and Victor had told me sooner, we would have been able to do something to control his condition.'

I stared at her. 'A tumour! Is that like cancer?'

'It's not cancer but he will probably need an operation. His blood samples have been sent to a specialist.'

'What do you call it, the thing he's got?'

Mum sighed and stared at her hands folded on the kitchen table. 'It's called Gigantism.'

* * *

That night, I lay in the dark listening to Bernardo sleep.

Listening but hearing nothing.

Bernardo didn't make a sound. No snores. No breathing, no nothing. I switched on my night light and looked down at him to check if he was still alive.

He lay with his head thrown back, his neck long and vulnerable, mouth open. His arm was flung out over the bedding. He had two duvets but his feet – with his new socks on to keep warm – still poked out beyond the edge of his mattresses. Fine black hairs curled on the bare calves above the socks.

My brother was sick.

He didn't look like much of a giant when he was asleep.

18
Bernardo

Andi. Not Amandolina. *Andi*.

'With an *i*,' she said. 'Don't forget. Especially at school. Nobody will know who you're talking about if you call me Amandolina.'

Ma and Uncle Will . . . *Mum* and *Dad* . . . had to work a shift at the hospital even though it was a Sunday.

Ma hugged me tight and whispered against my stomach, 'You'll keep an eye on your sister, won't you, Nardo? Look after her today?'

She was speaking so softly I had to bend low to hear what she was saying.

'Of course!' I couldn't believe she thought she had to ask me.

She was very stern with Andi, though. 'Remember, you're grounded,' she said as they went out of the door.

Andi shrugged.

As we settled down in the living room, I asked her, '*Grounded*? What it mean?'

173

Her forehead knitted together for an instant. Then she smiled. 'Oh, it's just Mum's way of saying "be good"! Shall we watch *Star Wars*, then?'

I nodded, even though I must have watched *Star Wars* a thousand and more times at Jabby's house. He played it in the background whenever I was over, just for the comfort of it. If it was Andi's favourite film too, then I was game to see it for the one thousand and tenth time.

There was something different about Andi as we sat on opposite ends of the sofa. She seemed restless, but in a good way – like there was a fire burning on the inside that made her glow on the outside. She probably didn't even know that she was smiling.

My mind was a hundred miles away. Nearly seven thousand miles away, to be exact. That's how far the Philippines is from England. Jabbar and I did the sums by looking up longitudes on Google and adding up the miles in between. It was a long, long way.

Jabby must have been so disappointed that the Giant Killers game was postponed. But it can't be long now before the Arena opens. It looked ready to go when he took me there.

Jabby, Jabby. Since I arrived in England, I'd been sorely tempted to pick up my cellphone and text him.

But it would cost too much money. 'Use it for emergencies,' Ma had said. 'International text messages are quadruple the cost. We'll get you an English sim card later.'

Jabby must have taken a special trip to the internet café to send me that email. He didn't own a computer.

There was so much I wanted to tell him.

I wanted to tell him about how the air was so cold, its little teeth nibbled on your bare skin all the time. How the atmosphere was so dry your skin sat tight on your face, like a mask.

I wanted to tell him how silent it was at night – no rogue roosters crowing, no barking dogs or arguing neighbours. And how beautiful London was, the rows of brick houses, the paved roads, the people all dressed up in shoes and coats and scarves, not a single one in bare feet, rubber slippers or rags – though the cold might have had something to do with that.

And I wanted to tell him about Andi.

I wanted to ask him, what could I do to be a proper big brother? Until today, it's been Andi looking out for me instead of the other way around.

If anyone could make a connection with Andi, it would be Jabby. Jabs would be the perfect basketball-mad big brother.

And then I winced because something thrust, hard, deep into my heart. I pressed a palm against my chest. But I knew it was nothing serious. Just a pang.

I was homesick.

It was noon in London. The Philippines was eight hours ahead, so it would be 8 p.m. in San Andres. This being Sunday, Auntie would have made lunch of some pork belly deep-fried in chicken oil so that the crackling popped like popcorn. She would have made soup with steamed milkfish belly, tamarind juice and swamp cabbage, seasoned with lime.

My mouth watered at the thought.

Uncle always complained that Auntie made far too much food on Sundays. But somebody was always sure to stop by later in the afternoon: Old Tibo and Flash Gordon, Sister Len-Len with the baby, Sister Lydia, probably with an armful of purple yam jars left over from the stall.

Jabby always turned up about four and headed straight for the fridge and any leftovers. By the end of the day it felt like the entire barrio had dropped by. And Auntie will be slapping Uncle on the shoulder with a smug expression, saying, 'I told you there's never too much. There's only too little.'

And then I felt something cold on my face

and realized that a tear had strayed onto my cheek.

I wiped it away quickly, glancing sideways at Amandolina to see if she'd noticed.

But she wasn't there.

19
Andi

I couldn't believe it when BOTH Mum and Dad announced they had shifts. On a SUNDAY? And then Mum gave me that look. If a picture could paint a thousand words, one of Mum's glances could paint an encyclopaedia. *You are in charge of Bernardo until we get back from work*, her glance said.

Bernardo just went all meek and mild. I think he said 'OK' about twenty times while Mum was giving me precise instructions on how to melt a frozen pizza for lunch. She was talking at Bernardo as she went out the door, *Yakatakabaka*. Brush your hair, wash your feet, cut your toenails. And Bernardo continued to nod like a car ornament. And then we sat in front of the TV and he was TOTALLY captivated by *Star Wars* like it was the greatest movie that ever was.

At lunch time I left Bernardo with his mouth open in front of the TV and baked the pizza, leaving it on the table for him to find. Then I grabbed my gym bag and crept towards the front door. As I passed the sitting room's wide-open door, I could see Bernardo sitting on the couch, his legs stretched out in front of him like two abandoned telegraph poles as he watched the scene where Luke Skywalker finally rescues Princess Leia and all she can say is, 'Aren't you a little short for a storm trooper?'

The door made a tiny click as I shut it behind me.

Mum and Dad shouldn't be working today. I mean, it's Bernardo's first Sunday!

This was not my fault.

But the thought of Bernardo all alone in the house gave me a twinge of guilt. Poor guy, he had a brain tumour and he'd only just arrived in a strange country, and already he'd been abandoned.

Shut up, Andi. You left a note, remember?

The note said:

Forgot I had to meet someone this afternoon. Pizza on the table.
Back before Mum and Dad return.
DON'T DO ANYTHING.

Bernardo was not the type to mind. He would probably eat the pizza and put another DVD on.

Wouldn't he?

20
Bernardo

I read Andi's note again.

It didn't tell me anything. *Back before Mum and Dad return.* What did she mean? Where had she gone?

I looked carefully around the kitchen. There was nothing to see but the pizza and the dark hole where the ceiling had crumbled after my bath overflowed.

A tiny knot of panic began to grow in my throat. 'Oh no, Amandolina.' I hurried upstairs, clinging to the banisters as my big feet slipped and missed steps.

'Andi?' I croaked. The knot in my throat made it difficult to speak.

Here I was, musing about how I could be a better big brother, chaperone, guardian, confidant . . . and then I somehow misplaced my sister.

My bedding lay where I had left it, carefully arranged on my mattress on the floor, with my pyjamas neatly folded on top.

Above my bed, Andi's was a wilderness of quilt and

pillows, all in a bright orange basketball print. The trousers and T-shirt she was wearing when we were watching *Star Wars* lay on the floor. She must have changed before leaving.

Automatically I picked up the clothes on the floor and started to fold them. But then I stopped. Perhaps Andi had left something, some clue in a trouser pocket. But what would she say about me looking through her things? I felt like a sneak but I decided Andi's safety was more important than my qualms about invading her privacy. I thrust my hand into every pocket. A stick of chewing gum. A few coins. Nothing useful.

I swallowed my guilt and looked through the pile of books on her bedside table. Nothing. I picked up the basketball duvet and shook it out. A scrap of paper fluttered to the carpet.

On the paper was a scribble in blue ballpoint pen:

Sunday, 2 p.m., courts, training.

Sunday. That was today. And it should be turning two in a few minutes. Under the writing was a hasty sketch.

It was a map.

21
Andi

I was feeling a bit sorry for myself when I got to the courts, what with Mum forcing me into playing Evil Sister and abandoning Bernardo to an afternoon of wall-to-wall Darth Vader on his first weekend in London.

But after a few minutes I stopped feeling sorry for myself and began to feel sorry for Rocky.

The Souls were pure and utter rubbish. They could not shoot.

The courts were just round the corner from our new house, on the edge of some playing fields near the hospital. It was just an asphalt space surrounded by high walls of plastic-coated chicken wire.

The team was kitted in metallic blue, with 'Souls' across their chests in black, their shorts swishing like skirts over their knees. I wore my plainest of plain Nike gear. I had no desire to attract more attention than necessary.

They kept yelling encouraging stuff at each other

like, 'Oh, bad luck!' 'Good shot, otherwise.' *Good shot, otherwise?* They sounded like characters from one of those really bad black and white dramas on TV.

Anybody could see that it had nothing to do with bad luck and everything to do with slinging the ball around like they were in a pie-throwing festival.

Did I really want to become one of these clowns? If I believed in magic, I would have felt like I'd wasted a perfectly good wishing opportunity.

Rocky wasn't even there. Mister Bouncy Dread-locks was late. I had to sit on a bench just outside the chicken wire for half an hour. I couldn't just join in until he came.

One thing was for sure: Rocky wasn't worried about height. One of the boys was my size – maybe shorter. He had a tiny moustache. Maybe he wanted to make sure nobody mistook him for a kid from the primary school. He took the ball down the court, doing all sorts of fancy dribbling, his legs flashing in and out like a pair of scissors.

But he couldn't shoot either.

Where did Rocky get these guys?

'Hey.'

'Rocky!' I jumped to my feet.

Rocky loped up to the bench where I sat. He wasn't wearing his Chicago Bulls kit today either. Instead, he wore a grey tracksuit that had gone slightly pink. It must have got into a hot wash with some red socks.

The tempo on the court slowed down as the boys began to eye us with interest.

'So.' He gestured at the team. 'What do you think?'

I sucked some oxygen in between my teeth. 'Well . . .'

'They may not shoot but they sure can handle the ball,' Rocky said. 'We're bottom of the tournament but you know what they say, it's not the winning that counts.'

If it's not the winning that counts, then what's the point of playing at all? But I didn't say that aloud. I just nodded and followed Rocky into the court.

'We're playing our last game of the league next week,' Rocky said. 'And we're gonna go out with a bang.'

The Souls nodded politely and mumbled, 'Hey,' as Rocky introduced me.

'Louie here is our point guard,' Rocky said, indicating the short boy with the tiny moustache.

Louie held out his hand and I reluctantly shook it.

He didn't let go when we'd finished. He winked at Rocky. I glared, but Louie just grinned. The other Souls giggled.

They thought Rocky was only letting me play because he liked me.

The realization curdled any pleasure of getting a game. My cheeks heated up.

We played a practice match. Rocky called himself for the Reds and called me for the Blues. As we slipped numbered bibs over our heads, Louie, who was going to point guard for my side, gave me a smarmy smile. Idiot.

The Reds won the toss. Instead of taking the ball down to their basket as quickly as possible, they *strolled* across the court. The Blues stood around sniggering. OK. They were having fun with the girlfriend. Rocky glanced at me with an embarrassed smile.

'Quit mucking about, guys,' he yelled. But Louie just blew him a kiss. The Blues fell over themselves laughing.

Instead of getting serious with them, Rocky giggled.

That did it.

I stole the ball off the Reds' point man and raced to

the opposite end of the court. I stopped at the three-point line and jumped. *Swish.*

You would have needed a poop scoop to scrape their jaws off the asphalt. Louie rubbed his eyes with his fists like he couldn't believe it.

Rocky collected the ball and passed it down the court. This time the Reds put some muscle into their passes as they ran to their goal.

But snatching the ball off them was not hard. I raced to my three-point line. *Swish.*

I turned. All eyes were on me now.

The ball rolled swiftly across the court.

'Red ball!' Rocky yelled.

One of the Reds picked the ball up. But he just stood there as if he didn't know what to do.

Louie gently took the ball from him and began to run towards our side of the court, his eyes seeking mine.

I hung back to see if he could sink it.

But as he passed me on the three-point line, he palmed the ball into my hands, jogging backwards to see what I would do.

I raised it in the air, aimed, and released. *Swish.*

Louie grinned and swung towards me, his hand raised high.

We high-fived.

Suddenly we were running and passing and stealing. Whenever the Blues stole the ball, they passed it down to Louie, who delivered it to me at the three-point line. Then I scored.

Swish. Swish. Swish.

No more 'Oh, bad luck!' and 'Good shot, otherwise'.

Louie was grinning so hard his moustache looked like it was about to fall off.

After a few minutes, the score was telling.

Reds: 0, Blues: 30.

Note: all thirty points were mine.

We were playing basketball.

Then Rocky, bless his dreads, tried to sink a long one from the far end. It was typical Souls, all muscle and no eye. The ball bobbled high, high in the air, and it was obvious from the moment he released it that it was not going anywhere near the goal.

And then, from nowhere, a hand reached up and plucked it from the sky and popped it into the basket, like a coin through a slot. And the Reds went wild, as if they had won the NBA Finals. And all I could do was stare with my mouth hanging open.

Because the helping hand in the sky? It belonged to Bernardo, beamed out of nowhere to the perfect spot by the goal.

22
Bernardo

It was habit, I guess.

How many times did I go through the set-up with Jabby? Jabby simply threw a high ball – he didn't even need to aim – and I stepped towards the goal at the last moment to tip it into the basket.

So when the boy with hair like a toilet brush threw that high ball, it seemed the most natural thing in the world to step into the court and tip it in.

Andi came marching over, her face a knot of fury. The number on her bib was blue, not red like the toilet-brush boy's, and I realized that I had helped her opponent score.

I wished that I had kept my hands in my pockets.

'Holy Mother of God, what are you doing here?'

'Sorry. Sorry. I came to look for you.'

'How did you know where I was?'

I showed her the scrap of paper with the map, and she snatched it away from me and crumpled it into a ball.

'I not know . . . I . . . I . . .' I tried to explain that I had not realized it was the other team's ball. That I had reached up without thinking. That it was a game I played all the time with Jabbar and . . . and . . . But my English came out slow and garbled and the look of impatience in Andi's eyes turned into worry.

'I told you not to do anything. Now I'm in deep trouble. I'm going to be GROUNDED for the rest of my life.'

Oh.

She wasn't worried about the point. She was worried that Mama would find out. Whatever the word *grounded* meant, it wasn't something to be pleased about.

The boy with the toilet-brush hair pushed in. His skin was the same colour as mine but he had a straight nose and light brown eyes. He came up to just below my shoulder.

'That was so cool! Thanks, mate!'

Andi's face was like thunder.

'Sorry about that, Rocky. Bernardo didn't mean to grab your shot.'

'No, it's fine!' the boy said, shading his eyes as he peered up at me.

'Goodbye,' I said, turning around and wondering

if I could find my way home without the map.

'Wait!' The toilet-brush boy looked at Andi, raising an eyebrow like he was expecting her to do something.

I bowed my head, afraid to say anything that might turn out to be wrong.

'Rocky, this is my brother, Bernardo,' Andi said.

My brother, Bernardo. I almost gasped, I was so surprised by the pleasure of hearing those words. I flashed a grateful look at Andi but she wasn't looking at me.

'He just arrived from the Philippines,' Andi continued. 'Bernardo, this is Rocky. He's captain of the Souls. Our school team.'

My brother, Bernardo.

But Andi had wiped her face of all expression, wearing a blank mask like a shield. It was the same blank face that she had on when Mama had scolded her about the leak. *My brother, Bernardo.* Did the words mean anything at all to her? I bit my lip.

Rocky tugged one of the corkscrews on his head. 'Holy Kareem, mate, you're tall!'

I said the only thing that came to mind: 'Kareem? Kareem Abdul-Jabbar, MVP, Lakers, 1985.'

'Right,' Rocky said.

What was I thinking? Talk properly, Bernardo!
'Pleased you meet me.' I held out my hand. 'My best
friend nickname is Jabbar. After Kareem Abdul-
Jabbar.'

Rocky took my hand and shook it. His eyes
widened a little as my hand enveloped his.

'Jabbar, huh? You guys like basketball?'

I smiled. 'Michael Jordan is my biggest fan.'

Rocky blinked.

'What Bernardo means is *he* is *Michael Jordan*'s
biggest fan,' Andi said. 'Bernardo's starting at Saint
Sim's tomorrow.'

Rocky lit up like a light bulb.

'So.' He grinned at me as if he was sharing a
delicious secret. It was the whitest smile I'd ever seen.
I glanced nervously at Andi. She had bent down to
tie her shoelaces, her face still rigid. 'So, Bernardo,
what are you doing next week? When can you start?'

I stared down at him and then at Andi, uncom-
prehending.

Andi's head jerked up sharply, the blank mask
slipping off so briefly that if I had not been watching
her, I would not have seen it. The corners of her
mouth wobbled like she was going to cry. Why was
she upset? What was wrong? What did Rocky mean?

Then Andi pulled the blankness back on. 'Start?' she said in a flat voice.

'Yeah.' Rocky's smile seemed to become even whiter in the sunshine. 'Bernardo, you're the answer to our prayers. You're gonna win us the match next week!'

23
Andi

The Great and Wonderful Rocky, Captain of the Great and Wonderful Souls, says he can't allow me – shooting average: 100 per cent – to join his team. And yet he's perfectly happy to sign up a certain Big and Friendly GIANT even though it is obvious that he is in no shape to run or do anything that amounts to *proper* basketball – apart from being TALL.

If someone eight foot tall with sincere brown eyes ever makes you wish upon a stone . . . don't. Even if you don't believe in magic anyway . . . don't. Don't. Don't. Spare yourself the aggravation of something opposite coming true.

Rocky was so deliriously happy about discovering Bernardo that he seemed to think I would be deliriously happy too. Their last league game was on Tuesday, at home. Against a team called the Colts.

And he was going to play Bernardo.

No trial, no training, no nothing.

'Don't worry, mate, we just want you on the court for the first quarter. We're going to psych them out!' he chortled. 'So. Will you be in school tomorrow?'

'Yes.' Bernardo looked a little bit nervous. 'First day.'

'I've got a spare Souls uniform – you'll be fine in my kit. You're not as wide as you are tall,' Rocky said. 'The shorts might be a little bit short, but it won't be too bad. I'll bring it tomorrow.'

'I don't knows,' Bernardo said, looking at me as if I knew the answer to the meaning of life.

I looked away and shrugged.

Rocky slapped him on the shoulder. 'Bernie, mate, you'll be fantastic!'

As we walked out, Bernardo said, 'I carry for you.' Rookie of the Year grabbed at my gym bag but I hung on to it like a mother defending her young.

'I can MANAGE,' I replied with a vehemence that had Bernardo staring down at me with that puzzled, lost-puppy look that must have taken years to perfect.

'What wrong?' He said it so softly, so sympathetically, so perfectly.

'NOTHING.' I summoned all my will power to flatten my eyes, my nose, my mouth, flatten my face into nothing. Like a pancake.

And I walked a little bit faster, knowing that those tree trunks he called legs would not manage to pick up enough speed to catch up.

It was exactly four-thirty when I finally turned the key in the front door lock, Bernardo shambling up behind me. The reason I knew that was because my mobile beeped and I saw the time as I read the text message from Mum.

WER R U?!!!

And before I could even push the door, it swung open with a horror-movie violence that made me shut my eyes in preparation for the hatchet in the skull, the arrow in the chest, the bullet in the forehead. But it was just Mum, and she didn't need any weapons to smash against my head because she opened that door yelling, like her tongue had taken a running leap.

'Where were you? I came back early and there was NOBODY at home. There was PIZZA all over the kitchen table and Darth Vader on TV but no sign of you two. Andi, how many times have I WARNED you—'

'Mama, *I* am the blame.'

Bernardo stepped in front of me so hurriedly he almost lost his balance, but as he flayed about with his massive hands, I grabbed his arm and he steadied. 'I am the blame. Sorry, sorry, Mama.'

And then the two of them went into a *yakatakabaka* rant at the same time.

Bernardo managed to keep up his side, producing a forceful stream of Tagalog that crashed like heavy waves against Mum's rippling *yakatakas* until slowly it was only Bernardo doing the ranting and then he shut up a little and then bowed his head and said, finally, 'And I am the blame. Amandolina is not the fault. Very sorry, Mama.'

And incredibly, Mum pressed her lips together and stood aside and we walked into the house and had cold pizza for tea.

24
Bernardo

School was as alien as another planet.

It wasn't just because there were no nuns and no statues of saints in the corridor and no electric fans whirring on every ceiling and no children forming orderly queues the way we did at Sacred Heart Academy.

From the second Mama, Andi and I walked through the gates, it was clear that Saint Simeon's was a place with a different . . . attitude.

The entire student populace turned to stare at me of course.

But I was too busy staring back to care.

Although they were all younger or about my age, and although everyone was dressed in the green tie and grey flannels that was Saint Sim's school uniform, the children all seemed so . . . old. The boys were broad and tall, with hard faces, sideburns and stubble; the girls were all willowy and curvy and not afraid to show it. Everyone either had earphone wires dangling from their ears or were thumbing mobile phones or both. In one corner, there was a boy and a girl with their arms around each other.

Here I was, thinking that my peers at Sacred Heart were just as giddy as the next teenager. The nuns had stopped wearing the veil a few years ago, but Sister Mary John, who was in the habit of pulling at her veil when she was vexed, continued to pull at her short grey hair in the same way she used to yank at her veil. If Sister Mary John had to teach here in England, she would have ended up completely bald. Compared to Saint Sim's, the Sacred Heart boys seemed puny and beardless, and the girls doll-like and demure.

Mum and Andi took me to the school office, where we were met by a teacher named Mrs Green who said, 'Welcome to Saint Simeon,' and smiled even while she stared at my Tall Man T-shirt and Tall Man jeans with distaste. The school had agreed to let me wear my own clothes but Mrs Green clearly didn't approve.

She whisked me off so quickly that Mum barely had time to blow me a kiss and Andi only just managed to mumble, 'See ya, Bernardo.'

Mrs Green marched me along so smartly, my first impressions of the classrooms were fleeting flashes –

fancy electronic white boards instead of blackboards and chalk, loud laughter, computers everywhere, faces in doorways gazing at me in amazement.

How were my new classmates going to react when I stepped in through the door? Would my legs fit under those desks? Would they laugh at my broken English? I had not slept a wink the night before, worrying.

But then I realized that all my anxiety had been pointless. Mrs Green led me straight to an empty classroom and sat me at a table – and yes, I could get my legs under it because Mrs Green found a lower chair for me to use. And then it was multiplication and long division and sines and cosines and geometry and radius and pi and wind speed and vectors and . . .

It took hours. 'Aptitude tests, Bernard.' Mrs Green smiled her tight little smile. 'We want to know where you're at so that we can place you in the right classes. You might need some additional work on your English but I can see that you have no problem whatsoever with the maths. Well done.'

But it was hollow praise. My fingers ached from writing. Surely my eyes were crossed from staring at papers. And I couldn't feel my feet, I'd been sitting in the same position for so long.

'Ma'am?'

Mrs Green looked up from the papers she was marking, the smile still attached to her face like a brace. 'When does I go to my classroom?'

'*Do*. When *do* I go to my classroom.' Mrs Green's smile didn't waver or change, even when a bell somewhere far away rang. 'Tomorrow you will meet your classmates and form teacher. For now you need to complete these tests.'

'That bell is for recess time now?'

'We don't call it *recess* in this country. We call it *break*,' Mrs Green said. 'But no, that's the lunch bell. The morning break happened ages ago. Shall we go to the lunchroom?'

I had to eat with her? I smiled pleasantly, fighting to keep the horror from my face. 'No thanks you very, very much, Mrs Green. I finds my sister now.'

The smile slipped, like a picture frame gone crooked on the wall. Mrs Green's mouth pursed into a thin lipless line. 'That girl. She'd better not be in the gym again.'

Andi was in the gym.

Rocky was there too, his spare basketball kit in a plastic bag.

I slipped Rocky's kit on over my clothes. It fitted.

'You're actually really skinny in spite of your height,' he said, stepping back a few paces to look me up and down. 'You'll pass.'

The truth was, the shorts didn't quite reach to my knees. But at least they weren't riding up my thighs like those micro shorts worn by players from yesteryear. The fashion for long, long basketball shorts and tops meant that the kit hung on me in a way that was, if not right, at least not wrong.

I gave Andi a sideways glance. She was staring studiously past the free-throw line, at the small white notice by the front door, *No Entry Unless Authorized*. A basketball sat at her feet.

'OK, Rocky,' I said, holding out my hand.

Rocky shook it vigorously.

'OK. Fantastic! Tomorrow, we play ball!' Rocky grinned and turned to Andi. 'And you're coming to the game, I hope?'

The corner of Andi's mouth twitched and she looked up with startled eyes. 'Huh?'

'Tomorrow. Right here. Lunch time. Are you coming to see your brother's debut? It's the last game of the season, you gotta come!' Rocky said.

'Oh!' Andi said. 'Yeah. Yeah, of course.'

But she was looking everywhere except at him.

So I knew she didn't want to go.

As soon as Rocky left us, Andi turned silently to the goal. She picked up the basketball and began to shoot.

Thunk. The ball hit the ring and bounced away.

I carefully took Rocky's basketball kit off and tucked it into my backpack.

Andi ran to retrieve the ball and tried again. *Thunk.* Another miss.

It was only when she had missed a third time that I noticed the redness in her eyes, the sheen of tears on her cheeks.

'Andi?' If only I had the English, I could say, *Andi, what is wrong? Can I help? You can count on me. I'm your brother and I've loved you for ever and ever.* But it wasn't going to come out like that, was it? I was useless.

'Andi?'

Andi picked the ball up and hugged it like it was a teddy bear. She turned to me.

'It's not your fault, Bernardo,' she sighed. 'None of this is your fault. It's just bad luck.'

Andi was small but she was one of those people

who gave the impression of packing an explosion of energy within her tiny frame. I swear it sometimes felt like *she* was taller than *me*. Now, as she rubbed her eyes on her uniform's shirt sleeves and clutched the ball for dear life, she looked like a little girl. Her chin rose and her eyes looked directly into mine.

'Look, I was disappointed when I found out that the Souls were boys only. But they let me train with them, which was cool even though they're hopeless at basketball. I was just taken aback when Rocky decided to sign you up. I couldn't help feeling disappointed. I wished I was *you*.'

Andi wished she was me? I opened my mouth to speak but nothing came out. How could *anyone* wish that they were *me*?

I cleared my throat. 'I will not play,' I said. 'It is wrong. They only want . . .' I searched for the English word for 'sideshow' but it eluded me. 'Gimmick. They only want gimmick.'

Andi smiled, though tears continued to trickle down her face. 'I wish someone wanted *me* to be a gimmick on their team. It's not wrong, Bernardo. At least it's not wrong if you *want* to play. *Do* you want to play?'

I looked at Andi and suddenly I could see how

much *she* wanted to play with the Souls, how much basketball meant to *her*. And me playing was the closest she would ever get to being in the team. At that moment, I wanted to play. For Andi.

'Yes, yes, I will play,' I said.

'I'm glad.' Andi sighed and smiled. In the shifting light, the amber in her eyes changed to a greeny brown. 'That would be so cool, Bernardo.'

I smiled. 'My best friend. He want me to be . . . he want me to be gimmick for his team too.'

'Is that the friend who calls himself Jabbar?'

'Yes. Jabby. Short for Jabbar.'

'Such a cool name,' Andi said. And I could see that she meant it.

So I told her about Jabbar and the Arena and the Mountain Men and the Giant Killers.

25
Andi

When we emerged from the gym, my head was buzzing with Bernardo's story.

How Jabby had tried to cash in on his friend by organizing a game with a team called the Giant Killers. Telling it, Bernardo went red, his eyes wet and his voice gruff, reliving the upset again.

He didn't like being treated like a freak.

So, if he wouldn't let his best friend exploit him, why was he letting Rocky do it?

I was suddenly aware that a bunch of kids were watching us from the brick arch to the primary school that adjoined Saint Sim's.

They stayed carefully in their playground – primary kids weren't allowed into the secondary playground and these guys looked about seven or eight.

They giggled as they eyed up Bernardo.

'Hello!' One little boy waved, a big grin on his face.

Bernardo smiled back and waved shyly.

The children sniggered and whispered amongst themselves and the boy quickly detached himself from the crowd.

Looking over his shoulder to make sure their play-ground supervisor didn't see him, the boy crossed the primary boundary, ran up to Bernardo and kicked him on the shin.

Bernardo yelped and momentarily lost his balance. I steadied him with one hand and made a grab for the little monster with my other. But he'd already rejoined his cohorts at the arch and they were sniggering like hyenas and making faces at Bernardo and chanting.

'SHREK! SHREK! SHREK!'

The nerve! I was just about to lunge at them when I became conscious of Bernardo's hand on my shoulder.

He had a big smile on his face even though he was bent over, rubbing his leg.

'No, no,' he called to the children, his voice friendly. And he mimed a pair of horns on his head. 'Not Shrek! Shrek is *ogre*. He have horns!' Then he beat his chest like Hercules. 'I am GIANT!'

The kids laughed their heads off.

I clenched my fists but Bernardo's hand was firm

on my shoulder, urging me away. He waved and they all cheered and waved back.

Then the lunch bell rang and Bernardo returned to Mrs Green and I went to my next class, my thoughts in turmoil.

While Bernardo had been talking, I had stared hard at his face. It's funny how you could spend time with someone and not look closely at him. I mean, really *closely*.

With Bernardo you looked everywhere but his face.

Mostly because he was so tall, there was so much to take in.

But also because you were afraid of what you might see.

It's like when Coach, from my old school, had an accident with his bicycle and came in with both eyes reduced to massive bruises and his nose in a fat bandage which came off later to reveal ugly swelling that turned his snout into lumpen blue rock. Suddenly none of us could look him in the face. We were afraid our eyes would linger on his deformities. We were afraid we would be disgusted by what we saw.

Anyway, this was the first time I'd had a proper look at Bernardo.

And what I saw was a boy.

Just a boy.

And something more.

His face was soft, not yet a man's face or even something in between, like Rocky, whose cheeks plunged down in hard planes but without the broad jowly edges of an older man.

His eyes were soft too, beseeching puppy-dog eyes, searching, always searching. I could see Mum's short snub in his nose and the tilt of the other Bernardo's Chinesey eyes in his gaze.

But I realized with a start that our eyes were the same colour – hazelly, browny, with a sunburst of dark streaks and black pupils that magnified to deep black wells and shrank to tiny pinpoints with the changes in light.

Since he came, I had been conscious of Bernardo watching me when he thought I wasn't looking. It was creepy and annoying, but looking at him now, I realized with a start that he was waiting for something.

From me.

What was it? What did he want?

I knew things about Bernardo that Mum had told me over the years. That he broke his arm when he was four. That he loved pork crackling. That *Star Wars* was his favourite film.

I'd even talked to him on the phone once or twice a year. *Hi, Bernardo. Happy Christmas. Happy Birthday! How are Auntie and Uncle?*

But I didn't really know him.

I decided I should make an effort to get to know my big brother.

After school, I would ask him stuff about himself.

There was so much I didn't know.

26
Bernardo

I thought my heart would burst.

We talked from school gate to front door, from front door to kitchen table. We made a pizza, had some supper and then went upstairs to Andi's room and talked. The years of being apart seemed to fall away. I thought my heart would burst.

Andi asked me if I had any idea that I was going to grow so tall.

To answer the question, I had to tell her about Bernardo Carpio.

I had to tell her about Old Tibo, about how giants came to be.

I had to tell her about San Andres.

I had to tell her about Mad Nena.

And I had to tell her about Gabriela.

I was just thirteen and the smallest in my class.

That is not much of an excuse.

In fact, it wasn't an excuse at all because what I did

211

next was stupid in the extreme. Jabby would have been horrified if he knew. But I didn't tell him about it until afterwards.

All I knew was that I wanted to get back at Gabriela for what she and her gang did to me. Or maybe I was so upset that I wasn't going to London after all that I needed to take it out on someone.

I decided that I was going to take the wishing stone from Gabriela the way she and her gang had taken the packet of shells from me.

I was stupid with rage.

Gabriela and her mother lived several blocks from school, in a small house, its concrete walls finished to imitate adobe brick, its windows arched like terrified eyes. It stood out amongst the dull grey houses on the street because it was the only one with a coat of paint – thanks to Ruben the painter who thought his kidney troubles would return if he didn't do what Nena ordered him to do. So the house shone like a beacon, its gleaming whiteness concealing the black-ness within.

Gabriela always parted ways with her gang at the school gates and always, always went straight home. Three days in a row, I followed her home but turned back at the last minute. On the fourth day, I steeled myself. I had to do it. If I didn't get on with the task, I never would.

Outside was a sign, *Beware of the Dog*. I gritted my teeth. I'd forgotten about Judas, Gabriela's vile pet.

Under *Beware of the Dog* was another sign, *Trespassers Will Be Punished* – I don't understand why they bothered with the sign. It was like underlining the obvious.

Nobody in San Andres would dare cross their threshold uninvited.

Nobody would risk Nena's wrath.

Well, almost nobody.

I licked my lips. My saliva tasted bitter.

Nena had drawn a chalk line on the pavement around the house. At each corner of the chalk line she drew an upside-down cross. The message was clear. Anybody who crossed the line would be struck down by some unspeakable curse.

Did I believe it? If someone had asked me at the time, I would have puffed out my chest and said, no, it was pure superstition. The nuns at Sacred Heart were always lecturing us about avoiding false notions, like not washing your hair before going to bed for fear you will wake up a lunatic. Or never stepping over a sleeping child to avoid misfortune. Or witches and black magic.

'Just say no to superstition,' Sister Mary John warned. But it had always been easy to see that the nuns were as afraid of Gabriela and her mother as the rest of the barrio.

On the day, I did not allow myself to think. Revenge. I was going to have my revenge.

I edged around the side of the house and peeked in through one of the wide, arched windows. It was shuttered with a mosquito screen and the thick curtains within were drawn. I couldn't see anything.

But I could hear. There was a voice, raised and sharp. Nena. Gabriela's voice replied, calm and cool. They were arguing about something.

I pressed my face against the mosquito screen, my nose flattened against the mesh, trying to make out what she was saying.

Nena's voice kept on, slightly hysterical, high and insistent. Gabriela answered back, her replies cold and low, unfazed.

A door banged shut within.

Then silence.

I pressed my ear against the mosquito screen, cursing the curtains that prevented me from seeing what was going on inside. Had they left the room?

Suddenly the curtains opened wide.

I was so shocked I didn't even try to move away.

There was a flicker of surprise in Gabriela's eyes. But only a flicker.

She stared down at me coolly as I finally stumbled backwards from the window. I forced myself to glare at her, pretending a courage that I hoped would harden into some semblance of real nerve.

But my defiance shrivelled in her unblinking stare. My muscles tensed into knots. *Run, Nardo*, they said. *RUN!*

But I couldn't move.

Her gaze locked me in a thrall. I couldn't look away.

'Gabriela, did I hear you open the curtains?' Nena's voice was muffled. She was elsewhere, in another room. 'How many times have I told you to keep those curtains shut?'

A smile played on her lips. *Run, run*, my body screamed. But still I couldn't move. It was as if my feet had suddenly grown long roots that tethered me to the ground under her window.

'*Putris!*' Her mother's harsh voice rang from the next room. 'I said shut those curtains!'

'Yes, Mother.'

But instead of drawing the curtains shut, Gabriela pushed the mosquito screens wide open and reached out. Before I could move away, she grabbed me by the shirt and dragged me over the low sill into the room.

I struggled, but she was stronger and bigger than me. She flung me to the floor, and as I knelt there, dazed, she quickly shut the screens and drew the curtains. Then she held me by the shoulders, a malicious smile on her face.

'Let me go!' I whispered.

Gabriela shoved me so hard that I tumbled backwards onto the floor. When I tried to get up, she slapped me on the cheek, contempt etched on her face. 'Stupid boy!'

She was whispering, which was a small comfort. She clearly had no intention of alerting her mother.

There was a thick odour.

Perfume?

No, incense.

An elaborately carved altar leaned against one wall, with fat candles burning on either side of a massive statue of Christ with one hand outstretched, on his bosom a heart wrapped in thorns. This Christ did not wear the tragic expression so customary of the statues that lined the walls of any parish church. This was an angry Christ – his eyebrows drawn together in a scowl, a snarl twisting the aquiline nose and a sneer curling his lips. The cold blue glass eyes embedded in the plaster face gleamed.

Hanging from the ceiling and along the walls were braids of garlic and all manner of herbs. There were whips woven from abaca and jars filled with multi-coloured powders, seeds and liquids.

A cold finger traced a path down the back of my neck.

These were the tools in trade of a witch.

'Yes, Bernardo, as you can see you're in big trouble.' Gabriela simpered.

Frantically I looked around for a way out. As if she could read my mind, Gabriela let go of my arm and closed the window latch.

Trapped! I edged away from Gabriela, who loomed over me like an evil shadow.

'Did you want those shells back?' She continued to advance as I backed away.

'Let me out of here.'

'I thought I fancied them but then I realized that I didn't.'

'Please.' My head bumped on the edge of a table

and I realized that I had backed into the altar. The angry Christ scowled at me from above.

'I threw them away!'

She threw them away? I should have exploded with anger but I was too terrified.

In the distance, I heard a sharp yelp.

'Bernardo, Bernardo. I wonder why you have come.' She clenched her fists and, without warning, drew back an arm to hit me.

I cowered and shut my eyes, raising my arms to block her blows. But they never came.

'Ah, maybe you're here to make a wish? Is that it?'

Slowly I opened my eyes.

'Is this what you want?' Gabriela stood there, swaying her hips, like a girl flirting with a boy. She toyed with the wishing stone that hung from her neck. 'Did you want my stone?'

I gasped. How did she know?

She lifted the wishing stone from her bosom on its chain and swung it like a pendulum. Malevolence twisted the pretty face.

'Idiot!' Her eyes flashed. 'You thought you could sneak in here and steal the stone! What were you going to do? Hold me down and rip it off my neck?'

I did not trust myself to speak.

'Or maybe you wanted to make a wish!' She thumbed the stone and grinned.

'I know! You obviously think you're some kind of hero. Some kind of Bernardo Carpio.' She closed her eyes and pressed it against her heart. 'Stone, let this pipsqueak turn into a Bernardo Carpio!'

Bernardo Carpio!

My mouth dropped open. She would have me turn into a giant? She was mad.

Suddenly the door flew open. Nena stood in the doorway, an ugly smirk on her face.

'*Putris!* Who is this?'

I saw the glimmer of alarm on Gabriela's face as she whirled towards her mother.

'You insolent girl!' Nena snatched one of the whips from the wall and advanced on Gabriela, fury etched on her face.

'Ma, I can explain!' Gabriela let go of the wishing stone and backed away. I realized with surprise that, domineering, outrageous and vicious though she was, Gabriela feared her mother.

This was my chance.

My only chance.

I leaped up, bumbling into the statue behind me.

The angry Christ teetered, and for a moment I thought it was going to fall on me.

In my haste to get out of the way, I blundered into Gabriela.

But the statue, weirdly, didn't fall. It righted itself.

'Grab him!' Nena screamed.

Gabriela snatched me up against her in a tight embrace. I found my face pressed against the black stone dangling from her neck. My hand closed around it and I pulled it hard as I lunged away from her clutches. The necklace snapped off with a tiny *ping*.

'No!' Nena's face was livid. 'Gabriela, he's got the stone!'

'Give it back, you little monster!' Gabriela, her eyes angry and staring, her teeth bared, looked more beast than beauty.

I ran for the front door.

There was a howl and I remembered with horror the sign on their front door. *Beware of the Dog*. Judas! *Oh please oh please oh please*. I could hear the dog's toenails clattering on the tiled floor behind me, its heavy panting interspersed with a ferocious growling.

I reached the door and my numbed fingers fumbled to undo the massive latch. Suddenly Gabriela was upon me, her long fingernails digging into my arms as she tried to tear me away from the door. We tumbled down to the ground, me trying to get away, Gabriela's nails biting into my hand.

Then the dog's wild barking was suddenly closer. It leaped on us and I could smell the stench of its breath, feel the heat of its body.

Gabriela screamed and let go of me. I didn't wait to see what had happened. I yanked the door open and ran out.

As I stumbled away, I looked over my shoulder. Gabriela's arm was caught fast between Judas' slavering jaws. The witch was there, frantic, pulling at the dog's collar. But the dog was not letting go. Gabriela screamed, struggling to get away. There was a mad, unseeing look in the beast's eyes as it shook the limb from side to side, the saliva foaming from its mouth stained crimson by Gabriela's blood.

I ran.

And as I ran, my courage shrivelled and turned black like a rotten banana.

Because after all that, I had failed.

I was such an idiot.

In the struggle, I had dropped the stone.

27
Andi

'**I** have sorry. My English is . . . *barok*.'
Barok. Baroque? Broken?

'It's OK, Bernardo, I understand everything.'

How many times had Bernardo apologized for his English? I couldn't seem to make him understand that it really, really was OK.

In a funny way, I think I do get a lot of Tagalog. Language is just like a film soundtrack. I've heard Mum and Dad say, *Hey, that piece of music was the soundtrack of my childhood!* Well. Bernardo's *barok* English was just him singing *his* soundtrack in another *key*. Not his key. My key. When I thought about it that way, it wasn't the funny, broken English that I heard but the story he wanted to tell.

And what a story it was.

It was so strange and wonderful and terrible and awful at the same time. It was so unfair. Poor Bernardo, the smallest in his class, just a boy. Going through all that. And us, his family, who should've been there with him, out here on the other side of the world.

How lonely he must have been. How he must have missed being with a mum and a dad – and a sister.

And I felt a sharp pang. Because I should have been there with him, shouldn't I?

The funny thing is that Bernardo and I have more in common than anyone would think.

And the truth is, even though I didn't know him, I have missed him just as much as he has missed me.

28
Bernardo

So I ran.

Ran from Judas, his sharp teeth sunk into Gabriela's white flesh.

Ran from Gabriela, screaming and fighting to free herself from the evil dog's grip.

Ran from Nena, the witch, trying to pull the dog off her daughter.

I ran all the way home, and that afternoon Auntie returned from the shops in a frenzy of gossip about how Gabriela was bitten by her own evil dog. How the neighbours had struggled to force the dog to let go. How instead of thanking them for their troubles, Gabriela and Nena had rushed back into the house, slamming the door behind them. How the dog was left outside the house, crazed and bloodthirsty. How everyone had fled into their houses as the dog had howled and snapped. How—

'Enough, enough, Auntie,' I cried, unable to bear

the horror of it all. 'I don't want to hear about it!' I ran upstairs to my bedroom.

I did not emerge for supper and stayed in my room until well into the next day. 'What is the matter with you?' Uncle shouted through the door.

'I don't feel well,' I replied. 'Please leave me alone. I just want to sleep.'

I was waiting, waiting for the police to come. Isn't that what Gabriela and Nena would do? Wouldn't they command the police to fetch me and put me into jail? But nobody came.

When I finally did venture out, I pretended that I had a splitting headache. Auntie gave me a Panadol and sent me back to bed.

And I waited.

And still nobody came.

After three days, Auntie made me go back to school. Of Gabriela there was no sign. She didn't turn up at school but that wasn't unusual. Gabriela took holidays whenever she felt like it, and everyone – the nuns, the teachers, the children – was always happier for her absence. I avoided all talk about the witch and her daughter. Whenever Auntie started, I walked out of the room. I didn't want to know because if I didn't know, I couldn't be held responsible.

But still I was afraid.

It was a month before I realized what was happening to me. A month! I had no idea. And by the time I noticed, it was too late.

One day I saw a house lizard above the old wardrobe in my room. Auntie hated house lizards; the sight of them sent her into hysterics. Without thinking, I had plucked the lizard from the wall and released it to a tree in the back yard. It was only when I returned to my room that I began to think. To fetch the lizard high up on the bedroom wall, I had not needed to stand on a chair. To release it, I had merely reached up to a tree branch.

I had grown a foot taller.

'But it must be normal,' Uncle said. 'Boys his age grow fast. I remember when I was his age, one moment I was a small boy, the next I was a teenager!'

I overheard Auntie on the phone to Mama. 'Hello? Hello? Mary Ann? Oh, that Bernardo, he's growing so fast.'

Everyone in San Andres acted like there was nothing strange about it. 'How you've grown, Nardo,' they said. But I lay awake at night, listening to my bones creak like bamboo as they lengthened. Wasn't that the way with giants? Had not Old Tibo told us over and over again? You needed to stand back. Up close you couldn't see them. Giants were the landscape.

I did not need to see a doctor. I knew what had happened. I was cursed.

I decided that I had to go back. I had to apologize. Then the growing would stop.

I knocked on Gabriela's door with a beating heart, my apology carefully memorized.

The door swung open and at first I did not recognize the woman who opened the door. Her hair was a tangle, like thick black telephone wires matted in a coiled mess.

It was Nena.

I tried to speak. 'Good . . . good afternoon . . .'

Her eyes stared into mine without any recognition. She was covered with a greasy-looking filth, like she'd been rolling around in the motor oil that dripped from the engines of the tricycles on the street. She smelled like she had not bathed for weeks. I took a tiny step back and resisted the urge to cover my nose.

'M-Ma'am?'

But the woman did not seem to see me. She squatted down on her haunches, muttering to herself. She might have been praying but I wasn't sure.

A hand touched my shoulder and I whirled around.

'Bernardo!' It was Sister Lydia, who lived down the road. 'My, how you've grown!'

'Sister Lydia,' I said. And then I couldn't go on. *What is wrong with Nena?* I wanted to ask. But my old fears locked the question in my throat.

Sister Lydia seemed unafraid. She stepped past me and bent down, gently helping the witch up to her feet. She spoke slowly to Sister Nena, like she was speaking to a child. 'There, there, darling. Go back inside.' She put a hand on Nena's elbow and tried to usher her back into the house but the woman just turned and pressed her face against the door.

Sister Lydia turned to me. 'She is sick. She's been very sick since the dog bit Gabriela. You heard about it, didn't you?'

'Yes, I heard.'

'And what did you want from Nena?'

I bowed my head. How could Nena free me from the curse in this state? What was I to do now? Perhaps Gabriela would know. 'Gabriela, is she here?'

As if in answer to my question, the dog began to howl inside the house, like a wolf at the moon. Goose pimples rose on my arms and I shuffled uncomfortably. 'Oh, that Judas. He scares me.'

Sister Lydia's eyes widened. 'Nardo, that isn't Judas.'

I squinted at her. 'What do you mean?'

'Judas was rabid. Dangerous. After he bit Gabriela, he went wild in the streets. We had to call the police. They caught him and destroyed him.'

'Destroyed him? Then . . .'

The dog's howls became louder. They were coming from the room above our heads.

Sister Lydia covered her face with her hands. 'The dog is dead. That sound . . . !'

There was a banging above our heads and a window swung open. The dog's howls resonated from deep inside the upstairs room. They subsided for a moment and then a shrieking began, unearthly and high and sharp.

Nena suddenly began to scream. 'Gabriela! Oh save her, Lord! Gabriela!'

She threw her head back and held both arms out at the window as if someone was going to leap into her embrace.

Only then did I notice the small face staring down at us from the window. The hair was matted in long unkempt strands. If Gabriela had ever been a beauty, it was hard to see. Her expression was contorted with pain and madness. She strained towards the window, grunting like an animal. And then she opened her mouth and gave another bloodcurdling howl.

'The dog infected Gabriela with rabies,' Sister Lydia said, gently putting an arm around Nena, who was sobbing into the wall. 'For a month, her mother tried to cure the illness with her spells and potions but nothing worked. By the time she took Gabriela to a doctor, it was too late. Nobody can help her now.'

29
Andi

Everything pales into insignificance.
I've heard that said; read it in books.

But when it fits something you know in real life. Well. Everything pales into insignificance. All our troubles. The shoebox house. The workaholic parents. The basketball, or lack of it. Everything paled in the face of what Bernardo had been through.

I am the blame. Bernardo's soft, sad voice echoed in my head like my brain had somehow vanished and the sentence was just bouncing around in my big empty skull.

Yesterday's Andi might have sniggered to herself – I mean, giants and witches and curses. I don't go for Harry Potter or *The Lord of the Rings* or . . . but what Bernardo's been through – it wasn't just about magic, was it?

It took Gabriela a month to die of rabies.
After her death, her mother became obsessed with

Saint Gertrude, who has the power to free souls from Purgatory.

'Mad Nena, she pray and pray so that Gabriela can go to Heaven,' Bernardo explained. 'Sometimes I pray too. I be very sad for her.'

I was tempted to say Gabriela did not sound like the Purgatory type. Wasn't Purgatory a way-station for sinners who could still be saved? I had no doubt that she went straight to Hell.

But the earnest expression on Bernardo's face made me hold my tongue.

On the day Gabriela finally died, Bernardo – who had grown to six and a half foot tall – took the bus to the nearest church in the next village, San Isidro. He went to Confession and begged forgiveness for his part in her decline.

Confession is supposed to be the secret sacrament, right? The priest, as God's stand-in, is sworn never to reveal the confessions of his people. That's how the slate can be wiped clean, and everyone can start from scratch and all that. Well. San Isidro had not been immune from the brutal bullying of the witch and her daughter. The priest could barely contain himself when he heard that Gabriela was dead and that the witch had lost her mind. He leaped out of the confessional and shook Bernardo's hand.

Soon villages up and down the hills of Montalban were buzzing with the news.

Everybody knew.

And that's how Bernardo became a hero.

He had freed the people of Montalban from the tyranny of Nena and Gabriela.

Turning into a giant was actually a sideshow to the whole thing.

The fact that the earthquakes stopped was a bonus.

That night, I watched Bernardo sleep his silent sleep.

His hand lay across his chest and his head was thrown back, his Adam's apple bobbing gently as he breathed.

My brother.

Home at last.

Things were going to be better from now on, I swore to myself. Bernardo didn't deserve to be treated like a freak. He didn't deserve to be treated like a stranger either. And I was going to be a great sister. At the game tomorrow, I would cheer for him until my tonsils fell out. And he was going to shock the Colts into a stupor and the Souls would play themselves to victory and it would be all because of Bernardo.

The door opened.

Mum's face appeared in the crack.

Our eyes met and she quickly shut the door.

There was something in her expression that made me jump out of bed and follow her out.

'Mum? What is it?'

I could hear the drone of the news on TV downstairs.

Mum turned away but not before I saw her flick tears from her eyes. My heart began to boom in my ears.

'Mum! Something's wrong? Is it Bernardo? Did you get more results back from the hospital?'

'No! No, it's not that.'

I pulled her shoulder round to face me. Her eyes were smudged from weeping.

'Then what is it?'

Her mouth trembled. 'It's not Bernardo – there has been an earthquake in the Philippines. A massive earthquake.'

I stood there, my bare feet suddenly rooted to the carpet. I had never felt so small and so helpless, the blood rushing about in my head like a wild river. 'An earthquake?' I had stopped breathing.

Mum's eyes were black holes.

'Montalban was at the epicentre. San Andres . . . it's been destroyed.'

Part Three

Wish Fulfilment

1
Bernardo

'Slam dunk!'

Jabby looked resplendent in a brand-new red, white and blue Mountain Men kit.

I laughed. 'You're not tall enough!' And he wasn't. Only players over six foot ever managed dunks.

Jabby looked hurt. 'Do you know the Americans banned dunking in the nineteen seventies?'

'So you've told me a million times.'

'And you know why they banned it?'

'Yes I do. You told me.'

'They banned it because Kareem Abdul-Jabbar, my *namesake*, was just too good! They banned it so other players could catch up!'

'Whatever. You can't do it, Jabby.'

'Watch me.'

And with that, he jumped, jumped from standing, without even a running leap, up and up and up, up beyond the ring, up to the rafters of the dome, up to the big round glass light, up like a shooting star, so fast that I thought he was going to crash right through and shower me with broken glass; but no, inches away, he peaked and then down he went, the ball raised aloft, muscles bulging, hard determination on his face.

And BANG.

He banged it in.

The ball shot through the basket and Jabby grabbed the ring, hanging on with a big grin on his face, swinging like a monkey, back and forth, back and forth. And then I realized that the whole stadium had begun to swing too, back and forth, slowly at first and then faster and faster and faster and faster, and then Jabby couldn't hang on any more and let go of the ring, and then he was falling, falling, falling.

'Nardo! Help! *Help!*'

I opened my eyes.

'Jabby?'

Even as I said his name I knew it was just a dream.

Andi's basketball duvet had fallen off her bed onto my face. Michael Jordan leaped high above me on the wall poster. Sunshine streamed in through the gap in the curtains.

'Andi?' I called up to her bed. But when I sat up to look, it was empty and the door was ajar. Andi was already up.

Slowly, morning noises drifted into my awareness. The TV's chatter from downstairs. The trickle of water in the bathroom. Birds singing outside the window. There was a buzzing noise, like a saw. Uncle Will – Dad – was sleeping off the night shift in the next room.

I sighed and lay back, my arms under my head. A dream!

It was Jabby's ambition to do slam dunks even though he was just five ten and not much of a jumper. He could list the names of all the NBA players under six foot who managed dunks on a regular basis and he spent hours practising and jumping around like a pogo stick. Maybe this was a portent of good things to come. Maybe Jabby was about to make a breakthrough.

I grabbed my cellphone from the side table and thumbed a text message to Jabby.

DREAMED U CD DUNK.

Then I remembered. The Souls game. It was today!

My stomach contracted and I sat up, my back suddenly cold with sweat.

The door opened. Andi was already in her school uniform. For a moment the amber eyes looked serious but it must have been a trick of the light because she

239

bellowed cheerily, 'Mum says get up, sleepyhead, today's your big day!'

I was in and out of the bathroom and down the stairs in less than ten minutes.

The TV's drone cut off abruptly when I got to the bottom of the stairs. Ma appeared in the living-room doorway.

'Good morning, darling!'

Her hair was mussed up, and there were tired lines around her eyes, which were red.

'Oh.' I searched her face. 'What's wrong, Mama?'

She rubbed her eyes. 'It's hay fever.'

'Hay fever?' I had never heard of hay fever. Perhaps she meant high fever?

She rubbed her eyes again. 'It's an allergy. I only get it here in England. In the summer. Never get it in the Philippines. Oh, I can't believe I've got hay fever now. It's not summer any more, for heaven's sake. My eyes are so sore!'

She led the way to the kitchen and put some eggs out to fry for breakfast.

Andi was already sitting at the breakfast table.

'Hey, Bernardo.'

'Good morning.' There was something overly bright about her smile. And the way she directed her gaze back to her cereal bowl was just a little bit too quick. I looked from Ma to Andi.

No! Stop it. What was wrong with me? Yesterday was a breakthrough! It felt like Andi and I had finally connected. I felt so close to her after we talked. So why was I now mistrusting everything I saw?

My Darth Vader ring tone began to play. I couldn't believe it. Somebody was actually *calling*!

I'd had a few text messages of course, but in all that time no one had phoned – all my phone contacts were from San Andres . . . and nobody in San Andres could afford overseas calls. It was so pointless having the phone that I'd left it on a shelf in the kitchen and forgotten about it.

I picked it up and did a double take.

Mum eyed the phone.

'Is it from the Philippines?' she said.

'I had a missed call last night. From Jabby!'

'Is that so?' Mum turned towards the kitchen sink.

'And look, another call!'

'Jabby again?' Mum's voice was muffled. She was bent over the sink.

'Yes.' I frowned. 'Two missed calls from Jabby.'

But Mum was no longer listening, throwing water on her eyes and mumbling something about hay fever.

2
Andi

It had been a rough night.

Dad rushed in from work at two in the morning and the three of us watched the rolling reports on the twenty-four-hour news channel. The earthquake was a seven on the Richter scale, which is as strong as they come, and the village was so close to the epi-centre, the place was totally destroyed.

Dad and I sat on the sofa, shoulder to shoulder. We could not take our eyes off the screen. And even though we had the heating on full blast, my hands were freezing.

Mum, frantic and sobbing, worked the phones, trying to get through to Uncle and Auntie, but of course there was no answer. All the lines were down. The news helicopters were not able to land for hours, and when they did, everything was still in such chaos, nobody could tell them anything. Then the army arrived and soon there were scenes of trucks filled with men and women carrying children, and dogs and goats and chickens; and then the soldiers began to pull people out from under broken buildings.

One news crew stayed in an emergency room, and kept a tally of the casualties arriving. Fifty, one hundred, two hundred. The figures climbed by the minute.

Then tents began mushrooming in fields and there were doctors with surgical masks and nurses and bandages and splints and plaster casts.

And all the while Bernardo slept.

I was all for waking Bernardo up so that he could keep watch with us, but Mum shook her head.

'No, no, don't tell Bernardo anything.'

I stared at her. 'That's crazy, Mum. We've got to. Besides, it's unfair.'

Mum took my hand. 'Look, we will tell him. But not yet. First, we must make sure your Uncle Victor and Auntie Sofia are all right.'

All right? It was a gentle way of saying 'not dead'.

Mum's brown skin had a pale yellow cast, like the night had sucked some of the blood out of her.

'. . . and whatever we find out, I need time to pull myself together. And I want to choose my words carefully. It's . . . it's just too awful. I don't know how to tell Bernardo what happened.'

And she suddenly looked so tiny and so sad that all I could do was put my arms around her.

Poor Mum. Poor Bernardo. The villagers had tried to stop him from coming to England, hadn't they? They believed that without Bernardo, they were doomed. And now . . . and now . . .

Mum was right. Bernardo didn't have to know just yet.

My brain was a hive of buzzing as Bernardo and I walked to school. I could barely hear him talking for the swarm in my head, but I could have won a Best Actress trophy for all my laughing and smiling, strolling along as if I didn't have a care in the world, as if I hadn't spent the night watching a horror story unfold on the other side of the world, as if my heart had not turned to lead.

We were almost up to the school gates when Bernardo suddenly stopped.

'Andi! I forgets the uniform of Rocky.'

'Oh no,' I said, still acting to the hilt. 'You'll have to play basketball naked!'

Bernardo grinned. 'No, no, I just go back. There is many time.'

I slapped him on the arm, maybe a little bit too

heartily. 'And don't you dare try to get out of the game.'

Bernardo waved as he turned back towards home. 'Why I do that? Nothing will stops me from playing.'

3
Bernardo

Ma had given me my own key.

I didn't knock or ring the doorbell. Ma was on the night shift and she would be resting upstairs. Uncle Will was probably asleep as well. No point disturbing them. I crept in as quietly as I could.

The TV was on. Was that the news? I thought the breakfast news ended after nine o'clock in the morning.

I called out in Tagalog, 'Mama! Would you believe Andi and I went all the way to school before I realized I'd forgotten the basketball kit!'

I poked my head into the living room. 'Ma!'

But Ma wasn't there.

'Ma! Are you upstairs?' I called. But the volume was turned up so loud she couldn't possibly have heard me.

I glanced at the screen and froze.

Mad Nena.

Her face filled the screen. The eyes empty. The lips

246

moving. There was a news commentary over the shot but I could read her lips repeating the one word. *Gabriela. Gabriela. Gabriela.*

The camera zoomed out.

At first I thought it was some sort of scrap heap or a messy lumberyard or a garbage mountain. But no. The scraps of corrugated iron that lay broken over everything were once rooftops. The blocks of broken concrete were once walls. The shrouded figures on the ground . . . were once people. There was an army truck full of survivors, their faces bruised, their clothes covered in grime. A woman cuddled a tiny baby, her face expressionless. Was that Sister Len-Len?

It was as if my knees had suddenly turned to water. I grabbed at the door frame to stop myself falling. But I missed and landed hard on my elbow.

I crawled up to the TV on my knees. *I'm sorry, I'm sorry.* It was a long moment before I realized the voice whimpering was mine.

The commentator droned on over more pictures of crumbled buildings, trees snapped like twigs, bodies. I searched the faces of the people being interviewed. Auntie? Uncle? Old Tibo? Jabby?

But I didn't recognize anyone else.

San Andres was not the only village hit by the earthquake. I recognized San Isidro. Camachile. Santa Rita. All of Montalban had been reduced to ruins.

The commentator chattered on but only one word rang clear in my head.

Earthquake. Earthquake. Earthquake.

What have I done?

4
Andi

Saint Sim's was the usual.

Everyone was laughing and talking and comparing MP3 players and copying each other's notebooks. You really wouldn't think, to look at the playground, that hundreds of people over on the other side of the world had just had their lives crushed by a horrible earthquake.

And the weird thing was, everybody probably knew about it. Everybody had glanced at the newspaper headlines or heard the radio in passing or glimpsed something as they changed channels on the TV. *Hundreds of Casualties in Massive Philippine Earthquake.* But 'hundreds' are not people, are they? And blank faces on TV are not people either.

I shook myself. Andi, I told myself sternly, *don't think about it. Don't drive yourself crazy. Think about something else. Think about basketball.*

Huh. Basketball.

Bernardo was telling me this morning that high

school league basketball in the Philippines had such a following that it was shown on television. And the team captain was a hero. And not just the whole school but the general public and the sports press turned out to watch all the games, and there were cheerleaders and drums and blaring horns.

It's not quite like that in London.

The Americans invented basketball. So it couldn't compete with English sports like cricket, football and rugby. But then school cricket, football and rugby didn't make it to TV either.

That's why even though the new gym was smart and had all the right lines, it wasn't designed to have an audience. In fact, there was barely enough room for the players to sit on the sidelines, let alone cheerleaders.

And yet.

When I walked into the gym at lunch time, the gym endlines were crammed so full of sixth formers that the referee had to patrol the sidelines, threatening anyone who stepped over the boundary.

Rocky waved cheerily from where the Souls were bouncing up and down on the end line, eager to get on with it. 'Andi! Andi!'

I hurried over. 'Rocky, this is massive!'

Rocky winked. 'I spread the word in the sixth form that we were going to blast the Colts with a secret weapon.'

'Secret weapon? You must be kidding!' Bernardo was their secret weapon? Bernardo was purely decorative. Weren't they planning to, erm, shoot some balls as well? Score some goals? Isn't that how you win a game?

Rocky grinned. 'Shock and awe. We're gonna shock and awe them with our giant.'

Louie suddenly appeared. He threw an arm around me as if we were best friends for ever. Someone made loud kissing noises. Lucky I couldn't see who it was because if I had, he wouldn't have been able to crawl on the court once I'd done with him.

I shrugged Louie's arm off, my nose wrinkled. His uniform was already drenched with sweat and the game had not even started yet.

'Man, look at that giant!' someone said and the crowd erupted in cheers and whistles.

'Here he comes!' Rocky said and we all turned towards the entrance, expecting to see Bernardo towering over the crowd.

But instead of Bernardo, the Colts made their appearance.

And leading them was a giant.

Well, he wasn't a giant like Bernardo. He was *tall*. *Properly* tall.

But where Bernardo had string beans for arms, he had rocks bulging under his skin. His chest was hard and massive. And when he moved, parts of him *rippled*. Rambo without the guns.

If Rocky thought Bernardo was going to shock and awe the Colts, he was mistaken.

I glanced at the Souls.

They looked shocked.

And awed.

So did the spectators.

The Colts jogged onto the court. The rest were tall too. Trees with hairy legs. They were not as tall as Bernardo but he would have looked like a joke standing next to them.

They began a warm-up shooting drill.

Swish. Swish. Swish.

Not a single miss.

Rocky swallowed.

5
Bernardo

I closed my eyes.
Please, please. Make them safe. Make them safe.

Auntie Sofia.

Uncle Victor.

Jabby.

Old Tibo.

Please. Please. Please.

But the wishing stone lay in my hand, inert.

No spark.

No heat.

No life.

Grant me this wish.

Please. Please.

I pressed it against my forehead.

It was smooth and hard and cold.

So cold.

I dropped it on Andi's bed and leaned weakly against the bed frame.

Downstairs, I heard the Darth Vader ring tone go off again.

I made my way down.

It flashed on the shelf. After the missed call, I had plugged it in to recharge. The ring tone had extra urgency.

It stopped ringing as soon as I picked it up. There were five missed calls now.

They were all from Jabby.

6
Andi

It was a disaster.

It was a massacre.

The Colts *owned* the Souls.

No sooner had the Souls gained possession of the ball than one of the Colts plucked it away and passed it down to Rambo, who reached up and STUFFED it in the basket.

Stuffstuffstuffstuffstuffstuffstuff.

Rocky was running up and down the court like a headless chicken and Louie was a waterfall of sweat, which was kind of ironic, considering he barely got a chance to run with the ball. When they did get the ball, they only managed to skim the basketball hoop or hit the referee or throw it into the crowd – throw it everywhere but into the goal.

The crowd watched silently. You could feel them clench their teeth every time the Colts' ball plopped through the basket and they cringed en masse every time the Souls missed.

Stuffstuffstuffstuffstuffstuffstuff.

The Souls were so dead.

But it was not the game that was worrying me.

Bernardo had not turned up.

Where was he?

Maybe he'd got cold feet. Maybe he'd seen the Colts and realized the futility of it all. Maybe Mrs Green was keeping him prisoner in the school somewhere. Or maybe . . . maybe he'd heard from the Philippines.

I began to shoulder my way through the silent crowd.

We should have told him. We should have called him downstairs last night. We should have stayed at home instead of going to school to play a stupid basketball game.

Mum was so wrong not to tell him about the earthquake.

Bernardo would blame himself.

I burst out of the gym double doors, panting. I needed to find Bernardo, but how? Where was I going to start?

My mind was a blank.

'Andi!'

The tall thin figure crouching behind the double doors straightened up hastily.

'Mrs Green?'

I stared, incredulous. She must have been watching the game through the glass panels on the doors.

Mrs Green's cheeks glowed red but she quickly masked any embarrassment with her usual tight smile.

'Mrs Green . . . have you seen—'

But she interrupted. 'Andi, I was very sorry to hear about the earthquake yesterday. I hope your family in the Philippines is safe and please let Bernardo know that I totally understand if he didn't feel like coming to school today—'

'Isn't Bernardo with you?'

She looked nonplussed.

'Why, no. He didn't come in this morning. I thought he didn't come in because of the – because of the—'

The doors burst open.

'ANDI!'

It was Louie.

'Rocky sent me to get you.' He bent over and pulled his shirt off in one movement. It was soaking and the sparse triangle of hair on his chest glistened with sweat.

'Louie Robins, put your shirt on this minute!' Mrs Green reached to grab the shirt.

But Louie wouldn't let go. 'Andi, they're KILLING us out there. We need you!'

I stared at him. What did he mean?

Louie stamped his foot like a toddler who'd been refused a sweet. 'ANDI!'

Mrs Green put her hand on his shoulder and shook him. 'Louie, explain yourself properly. You're not making sense.'

But he was so beside himself he just waved the shirt at me.

Mrs Green peered at him like she was examining a cockroach on the wall.

'I don't understand . . .' I stuttered.

Louie began to pull his shorts off. There was a blue Smurf pattern all over his boxers. I was so shocked I didn't even think to snigger. Instead of stopping him or averting her eyes, Mrs Green snatched the shorts and shirt away from him and grabbed my hand.

'Mrs Green!'

'Quick, to my office, it's just round the corner.'

'But . . .'

She glared at me.

'Andi Jones, are you not paying attention? The Souls need you. You are going to put on Louie's uniform and save that game.'

7
Bernardo

*J*abby. *Jabby.*

    Icy sweat trickled into my eyes. I fumbled with the phone. Call him. Tell him it will be OK.

    Do you need help, Jabby? Where are you?

    But my fingers scratched uselessly against the keypad, grotesque claws, my hands were twisting, curling, hardening. The phone fell to the living-room floor with an obscene clatter.

    It was happening again.

    Ma, where was Ma? *Ma, help!* But my vocal cords produced no sound.

    I was bent down, down, the world riding my back again. And there was a shrill screeching noise, like a thousand bats ejected from deep inside a cave. And I realized it was humankind shouting in horror . . . because I was buckling under the weight, it was so heavy; I could not hold it up, and the Earth was falling.

    It slid down my back, quivering like a giant jelly.

Earth and rock, tree and root crumbled through my wooden fingers.

Down, down.

It landed on the ground with a great *crack*, red tongues of flame licking out of the fractured shell.

And the screeching became higher, sharper, thinner, piercing my eardrums like a knitting needle.

8
Andi

It had worried me at first. At one point, Mum actually apologized. 'Andi, I didn't change shape until I was fifteen. I'm sorry. It's in our genes.'

All the girls my age were wearing junior bras and training bras and crop tops. They had all grown hips and bumpy little chests while I had remained as straight and flat as a plank.

Or a boy.

So Louie's basketball kit fitted me perfectly.

'Are you ready?'

I stared into the mirror in Mrs Green's office and tried to ignore the fact that the shirt was soaking wet with Louie's sweat and pungent with Louie's smell.

Mrs Green's reflection gazed at me critically from over my shoulder.

'You need something. Something to make you look less like a girl. Give me a second.'

She began to rummage through her desk, opening and closing drawers.

I pretended to examine myself in the mirror. But I was really studying a framed picture hanging next to it. It was a group picture of a girls' basketball team. The teenage girls in the picture had weird blow-dried hairstyles from some long-ago era. In the front row, a ball clasped in front of her, was a young Mrs Green, the tight little smile unmistakable in the smooth face, the short iron-grey bob replaced by a blonde perm. In a discreet little frame next to it was an auto-graphed photograph of Michael Jordan. *To my biggest fan*, it said.

Mrs Green, a basketball fan? Was that why she always just happened to be prowling around the gym, catching me out? Maybe she was shooting hoops when nobody was looking!

'Here.' She held up a tube of hair gel. 'Confiscated this from one of the girls the other day. Some children cannot tell the difference between a classroom and a hairdresser's. I'm sure she won't mind donating some to a worthy cause.'

She squeezed a dollop onto her hands and began to muss my hair. 'There!'

It was rich, Mrs Green complaining about hair-dressers. The pointy hairdo may have been a bit naff but it wasn't bad. She had turned me into a short version of Tintin, but with freckles and dressed in a basketball outfit. She could probably get a job in a cheapo barbershop somewhere, hairdressing pre-pubescent boys.

'Put this on.' She handed me a headband.

I put it on. Now I looked like Tintin as the Karate Kid.

I turned to her. 'Mrs Green . . . I . . . uh . . .'

She whirled me round by the shoulders and pushed me towards the door. 'I've seen you shooting your magic three-pointers, Andi. Go and save the Souls.'

So I went.

And as I went, something crossed my mind.

When Bernardo had presented me with the wishing stone, I had wished I could play point guard for the Souls.

Now my wish was about to come true.

9
Bernardo

The Earth lay on the ground, a broken egg, yolk the colour of blood oozing slowly out.

And then there was a bright light. So bright. I tried to open my eyes but it scorched my eyeballs. I turned my face away.

'Pupils are dilating. Hello, hello, anyone in there?'

'Huh?' I tried to open my eyes. The light had gone away. A dark blur, eyes, nose and mouth moving in the shadows.

'Do you know your name? What's your name?'

I screwed my eyes shut. What was my name? The answer came slowly to my lips. 'B-Bernardo.'

'Bernardo! Good. Bernardo, you're in an ambulance. You collapsed. Don't worry, we'll get to the bottom of this. Your mum is here.'

Mum's voice floated in the distance. She spoke in Tagalog. 'I'm here, Bernardo. Just rest, darling. Don't worry. We'll be at hospital soon.'

But the Earth! It fell! And . . . and . . .

'NARDO!'

Suddenly Jabby's face was pushed up against mine. There was a bloody bruise on his forehead, yellow and violet with swelling. A fine grime covered his face. I could smell his sweat, his fear. Dirt crumbled from his hair. He coughed. 'Nardo, help. Help me.'

And then he tumbled away from me. I sat up, tried to grab him, tried to stop him from falling, but then there was only the paramedic, urging me to lie down again, and Ma, her eyes wide with alarm, hand over mouth.

There was a popping noise, like someone had burst a balloon next to my ears.

I cried out, blind with sudden, excruciating pain.

'It's all right, Bernardo,' the paramedic said. 'Lie back. Everything is going to be fine.'

But I felt like I was going to die.

10
Andi

'**Y**ou're dead!'

Whack. Rambo probably didn't mean to hit me. It was probably meant to be a secret little nudge. The way you do when you're panicking because someone's about to snatch victory from you.

It was Souls: 28, Colts: 30.

If Rambo could just unbalance me a little bit, get the ball back to their goal, they had a chance of scoring in the last minute, and the Souls would have no time to take the game back.

But Rambo was more used to nudging raw beef than pushing someone as tiny as me around. So he overestimated his strength.

I went flying.

'*FOUL!*' Rocky screamed.

The referee blew his whistle and the crowd went mad.

I had two free throws. It was only for a point each

but they were points in the right direction. I could tie the score.

Looking back, I don't know why nobody questioned my appearance on the court with Louie's name and number on my back. The referee must have been asleep or blind or both. And the Colts didn't even raise a squeak.

They probably took one look at eeny meeny me and thought, no problem.

And then it was too late.

Because. I. Don't. Miss.

The Souls knew the drill. They just had to keep feeding me the ball.

The Colts were big and burly but they were too dumb to work out that a small person like me would shoot from the three-point line. Over and over again, the Colts bunched up under the goal, waiting for one of us to come close enough to shoot, only for me to pound it in from far, far away.

Swish. Swish. Swish.

I was glad for the headband. It mopped up the sweat that dripped endlessly down my head, which was getting stickier and stickier as my perspiration mixed with the cheap hair gel Mrs Green had put on my hair.

Rocky's dreads were standing on end, the atmosphere was so electric.

As we took our positions for the free throws, Rocky sidled up. 'YOU, Andi-Pandy, are my secret weapon!' He grinned. I could smell the relief on his sweat.

Surely Bernardo would be here by now. Scanning the faces on the sidelines, I recognized some kids from my class, waving like demented fans. And Mrs Green was screaming at the Souls to get some boys down to the halfway line. She acted as if she was their coach.

But there was no tall dark head poking above the crowd.

Bernardo, where are you?

Something must have happened to him.

Rambo loomed just to my left. He smirked. 'No chance, pretty little boy,' he said. 'You'll screw up and then we're taking that ball.'

'Why don't you go and lift some weights?' I said.

Bernardo, not long now.

But when I took the first shot, I missed.

Thunk.

I missed! But I never miss!

'Told you.' Rambo grinned.

Suddenly the crowd hushed.

Bernardo, I'm coming.

I licked my lips. *Focus, Andi. Only one more minute and the game will be over.*

I released my second free throw.

Swish.

The crowd roared. 29–30!

Rambo charged, elbowing me aside to grab the ball. I stumbled but the referee didn't call a foul.

I skittered down the court, not even checking to see which of the Souls would retrieve the ball. There was no time. I had to be ready on the three-point line if we were to—

'ANDI!'

I looked round in time to see Rocky throw himself between Rambo and the ball, knocking it down the court towards me.

Stay cool. Stay cool.

The Colts galloped after it. They were steaming, desperate.

The ball bounced twice and then rolled slowly in my direction.

'*SHOOT! SHOOT! SHOOT!*'

The crowd was beside itself.

Stay cool.

I picked up the ball and released it in one swooping movement.

Bingo.

Three points!

Souls: 32, Colts: 30.

The Souls had won their first and last game of the season.

'Andi! Andi! You did it!' I could hear Rocky's voice above the pandemonium as the crowd rushed onto the court to congratulate us.

'Andi! Andi!' Mrs Green's voice rose above the crowd.

'Hey! Andi! Come back!' Rocky yelled.

But I didn't stop running. Out of the double doors, out of the school gates.

I kept on running until I got home.

11
Bernardo

'Your brother is here.'

The nurse nodded towards the doorway.

Brother? I turned my head slowly and peered through the fog of pain at the small figure in the basketball uniform.

'That my sister,' I whispered and the nurse made a small snorting noise before she turned away.

Andi rushed to my side. 'Bernardo!' I closed my eyes, the light was so bright. Raindrops trickled on my face. 'Oh, Bernardo, I ran all the way here. Mum left a note on the door.' The raindrops were Andi's tears, and they were falling fast.

I lifted my hand to point at the uniform and the gesture launched another shard of glass into my brain. My lips were parched. I had to force my voice through the dry sand in my throat. 'Why?'

'I played for the Souls. I was point guard. That was my wish on the stone, Bernardo. It came true.' I felt Andi's lips on my cheek. They were soft and cool and the pain seemed to dim just a little. 'And we won.'

I tried to smile, but smiling made the knife dig deeper into the base of my skull. 'You are so *galing*,' I whispered. 'So good.'

'You have to leave, miss.' The nurse put a hand on her shoulder. 'Your brother has to go into the operating theatre now. The surgeons are waiting.'

12
Andi

A nd then we had to wait.
Mum and Dad had been upstairs when he came home. They found Bernardo on the kitchen floor. How long had he lain there, unconscious?

The ambulance, when it came, had to call another ambulance to help them manoeuvre Bernardo out of the living room and through the front door. There was only room for Mum in the ambulance that took Bernardo to hospital so Dad followed in the other one.

When Bernardo woke up, his head hurt, his eyes hurt, his neck hurt, he could barely move. At casualty, they did some tests, ran all the scans again. By the time I turned up, they had decided to operate.

'How bad is it, Mum?'

It must have been bad bad. I could tell from the terror in Mum's eyes. Having retrieved Bernardo after all these years, she thought he was about to be snatched away again. Was it the tumour? Were they going to cut him open and take it out? She was beside herself, and getting any information out of her was impossible. And I couldn't get Dad to explain anything to me either. He was too busy wrapping himself around Mum, turning into a human firewall, trying to shield her from all the things that have to be decided and signed and approved before your child goes into surgery. Shield her from the possibility of grief. Shield her from the people too.

Mum and Dad knew practically everyone at the hospital, of course. Doctors and nurses and orderlies were constantly stopping to talk to us.

'Oh, is this your daughter?'

'So sorry to hear about what happened to your son.'

'Poor you, is there anything we can do?'

Nobody would leave us alone.

So in the end we went home. It would be hours before they let Bernardo out of the operating theatre, and anyway, it was two in the morning and we needed to get some sleep. As if.

When we got home, I rushed upstairs and looked wildly around my room. The wishing stone. It was lying on Bernardo's bed.

I picked it up and knelt with the stone clutched to

my heart. *Please. Please. Make Bernardo better.* If ever there was a time to believe in miracles, this was it. *Please heal the tumour.*

Then I knelt there for a long time. Willing the wish to come true.

But of course nothing happened.

Wishes don't come true.

Bernardo turning into a giant.

Getting my wish to play with the Souls.

It was all stupid coincidence, wasn't it?

I dragged myself to my feet, feeling foolish.

The stone lay cold and useless in the palm of my hand. I was such an idiot.

I ran downstairs, pulled open the front door, and threw it into the rubbish bin by the front gate.

When I came back into the house, Mum and Dad were standing like statues in front of the answering machine in the living room. Its lights blinked furiously, like landing lights on a runway.

Ten messages, the digital counter said. Clearly, the lines from the Philippines had unblocked while we were at the hospital and here, at last, was news.

But they just stood there, staring.

Dad put his arm around Mum.

'Go on, you have to find out,' he whispered gently.

Mum cringed.

I climbed onto the sofa, hugging my knees. I waited, my heart in my throat.

Mum pressed the button and screwed her eyes shut as if something was about to hit her.

'First message,' the brash metallic voice said. *Beep!*

'Hello, hello? Mary Ann? Can you hear me?'

It was Auntie Sofia.

Auntie Sofia told Mum that up and down Montalban, the earthquake had pounded villages to extinction. The land was reduced to rubble as far as the eye could see. Everywhere, too, death had swept away men, women and children. The Philippines wept for hundreds.

San Andres itself was flattened. It was as if a giant foot had descended from above and stamped on the village.

And yet San Andres was hailed as the great miracle of the earthquake. Because though not a single house was left standing and the dome of its idiosyncratic stadium had collapsed into itself like a boiled egg tapped too hard by a spoon, in San Andres lives had been spared.

Only one person was found to be missing.

'Who is it? Is it someone we know?' Mum had cried. And when Auntie answered, I knew right away that all that stuff about San Andres being a miracle had been a kindness. Auntie had been preparing Mum for some really bad news.

'Jabby? Oh no, no, no.' And Mum put her head down on the table and began to sob. Dad bowed his head and awkwardly patted her shoulders.

I stared into space. Bernardo loved Jabby like a brother and now he was gone. How were we going to tell him what happened? How were we—

That was when I heard it ringing. It was the theme from *Star Wars*. Bernardo's ring tone.

It was behind the fridge for some reason. I had to lie on my tummy and reach through a curtain of cobwebs to retrieve it. How did it get there?

Twenty missed calls, Bernardo's screen said.

I clicked through.

All of them from Jabby.

13
Bernardo

I didn't know, of course, that Andi found the phone.

I was busy, lying on two operating tables laid end to end to accommodate my length, my shaven scalp peeled away from my head as the surgeons probed for the source of my troubles.

I didn't know, but when I heard the story later, there was a strange familiarity to it, as if I had been there, as if I'd seen it all unfold with my own eyes.

It was the day the Arena would have opened, the day the Mountain Men would have played the Giant Killers. But of course things had not gone according to plan. The current contractor (was it the fourth or the fifth?) had insisted that half the building ought to be torn down because the foundations were substandard. He was fired and another contractor hired and then fired, and then suddenly they were all suing each other and there were newspaper articles about bribery and corruption and illegal building permits and . . .

It had turned into a huge mess.

That very day it was announced that the owners were finally washing their hands of the Arena. They were going to rip out its insides and turn it into a covered market. Wreckers were scheduled to come in a week.

Jabby was devastated. All his dreams of glory had amounted to nothing. His immediate reaction was to call me, and his cellphone was ringing before he remembered that I was in London and that the call was going to cost a fortune and anyway it was probably four in the morning on the other side of the world. So he hung up before I could pick up.

That was Missed Call Number One.

And then he thought there was no time like now and he had better make the most of the Arena's basketball court while it was still there.

And he thought of inviting one of the other boys, revealing his secret entrance, having a play . . . but no. There was still time before the wreckers came to dismantle the courts. He could show it off later. For now, he just wanted to enjoy having the Arena to himself. It was evening: there would be nobody there.

And that's why Jabby was in the dome when the earthquake struck.

The first time the Earth moved, he was so wrapped up in his thoughts that he ignored it.

To be fair, earthquakes had been so frequent in San Andres that most village folk paid them no mind.

And then the bright yellow sports floor jerked up as if some great creature had shrugged its shoulders underground.

Jabby stood very, very still and realized that the ground was continuing to move. The creature was travelling the length of the court in one long motion. The stadium gave a loud groan. *Snap!* The glass light at the very top of the dome suddenly exploded into a thousand brilliant shards. He threw himself out of the way, cowering behind the first tier of seats as glass fell in a deadly rain.

The ground continued to move and the building groaned again. There was a series of popping noises and, looking up, he realized that the window panes were breaking, one after the other. A long crack split the ceiling and pieces of concrete were falling away in huge chunks.

Suddenly the seriousness of the situation hit home.

The dome was cracking up. If he didn't get out, he would be killed. Jabby began to run.

He made it to the entrance of the tunnel by which he'd entered, when the dome collapsed.

He remembered a lesson taught by Sister Mary John, a long, long time ago, in a galaxy far, far away, when San Andres was still the rock-and-roll capital of the world (at least according to the Book of World Records). 'If you are caught indoors during an earthquake,' Sister Mary John advised, 'look for triangles.' Put yourself in a triangle and you might survive, she said. Stand under a door frame, under a table, under a sofa – triangles would give you some protection from a collapsing building.

Sister Beaulah had dismissed the theory. 'That was a hoax, Sister,' she'd argued with Sister Mary John. 'You are wrong!' And then they'd quarrelled while the class had fidgeted.

It was too dark to see anything, much less a triangle. Jabby groped along the tunnel wall towards the exit. *Only a few feet more.* Something groaned, and under his fingers he felt the wall bulge. *Hurry, hurry.* There was a roaring, rushing noise as, behind him, the Arena crumbled. *Just a few more feet.*

Too late.

Suddenly there was an animal roar and the tunnel collapsed. He found himself lying under a layer of rubble in total darkness. Pieces of concrete fell away from his face.

I'm dead! he thought. *I'm dead!* If this was death, it stank. Foul toilet smells wafted around him. A pipe must have broken somewhere nearby. The air billowed with concrete dust. When he breathed in, his lungs filled with grit instead of air. But his head seemed to be in some kind of space. He could turn his head right and left. Perhaps he had found his little triangle.

There was a crushing weight on his legs, and his shoulders, chest and ribs hurt. His left hand had gone numb. A sharp pain scythed up his right elbow. *I'm broken*, he thought. *My legs must be broken, my arm is definitely broken and my ribs must be broken too.*

And then he realized that nobody knew where he was. The only person he'd ever shown the secret entrance to was me. He had not told anyone where he was going, of course. Nobody was going to find him.

And then a tiny square of light appeared in the total darkness somewhere to the left. There was a beep. It was his cellphone, which had somehow fallen out of his pocket into the rubble, opening the most recent text message on impact.

DREAMED U CD DUNK.

My text message.

He could see the message by craning his neck. Pain flared hot and sharp up his arm at the movement, but he smiled.

And then he thought, *Bernardo, I think you've just saved my life!*

He only had to call me back.

Tell me to tell everybody where he was.

So he gritted his teeth and forced himself to move his broken arm towards the phone. The pain slammed into him in waves, and he actually saw stars. *There, I've done it. Probably severed my arm.* But when he checked he had only moved his arm a few inches.

It was going to be harder to get rescued than he thought.

In fact, once he got his hand on the phone, his hand was so rigid, he could not possibly dial or send a text message. He could not do anything that involved any kind of dexterity. *The only way I can dial is if the phone had buttons the size of platters.*

Then he remembered. He could press the green

send button. Pressing the green send button should call the last person he had dialled. That last person being Bernardo.

He closed his eyes and gritted his teeth, flexing his shoulder muscles (probably torn) to raise his hand and drop it haphazardly on the phone. Nothing happened. He craned his neck.

Call Bernardo? +63091703333, the phone wanted to know.

'Yes!' he yelled. And then, since yelling didn't seem to have any effect on it, he dropped his hand on the phone again.

It dialled.

The ringing was thin and distant in the little space. 'Hello? Hello?' he shouted.

But the phone was not finished. 'Pick up, Bernardo.'

There was a click. 'Hello? Hello?'

He craned his neck.

Call ended.

In a temper, he tried to grab the phone; he wanted to shake it until it begged for mercy, shake it and break it and stamp on it. But his arm would not do it, and the sudden movement launched a wave of pain so intense that he screamed.

He closed his eyes.
Try again.
And again.
And again.
As long as it took to get through.
Or as long as he could still move his arm.
Or as long as his battery held out.

14
Andi

'Try again,' I begged Mum.

'The Arena people said the dome was empty at the time of the earthquake. They said it was locked up. They were going to gut it and turn it into a market, you know. The wreckers are coming tomorrow,' Mum said. 'How could you be sure Jabby was at the dome? For all you know he was visiting one of his other friends.'

I looked at Mum. She was right. I didn't even know Jabby. All I knew was that Bernardo had told me he liked to play in the dome, unbeknownst to the contractors, unbeknownst to anybody. It was the logical place to look for him. But we couldn't organize a rescue operation on the basis of twenty missed calls. Jabby could be anywhere.

'Could you try the Red Cross again?'

Mum sighed. 'Look, Andi, they've got enough on their plates at the moment. Even if I got through, the

Red Cross are already stretched to breaking point. They weren't interested. I really don't want to call them again.'

'What about the army?'

'Andi!' Mum shook her head. 'There are hundreds of people who need help. The army wouldn't have the time.'

Poor Jabby.

Bernardo's phone was totally silent. No more missed calls. Time was ticking away.

That a miracle had happened in San Andres had not escaped the news. The TV was full of heart-warming stories about the only village to survive the earthquake, every report ending with a photo of Jabby in his Mountain Men kit. 'Sadly the miracle is marred by one casualty. Young Henry Montano is missing and presumed dead.'

It was not just that Jabbar was Bernardo's best friend. Bernardo felt responsible for San Andres. In a weird way, he himself had believed he could keep the village safe. *I am the blame*. If Jabbar was found safe and sound, surely then Bernardo would be free? He wouldn't have to spend his life worrying that he was responsible for an entire village's well-being. Because the village would have survived without him.

We had to keep trying. For Bernardo's sake.

'Mum,' I said. 'Call Auntie.'

15
Bernardo

It's dead, Jabby thought. *And I am dead too. Goodbye, cruel world.*

The mobile phone battery had lasted a long time. Long enough for Jabby to make twenty excruciating attempts to call me. But always the phone disconnected itself.

'Why? Why?' he raged at it. 'What's wrong with you?'

And then he harangued the phone, only stopping because his sand-blocked lungs could not summon up enough air for another shout. At one point, the pain in his arms and legs became so intense, he could feel himself surrendering, falling into oblivion. He was tired, so tired. It was tempting to slip away, close his eyes, stop feeling, stop the pain. But he forced his eyes open, even though he could see nothing. If he allowed himself to sleep, he was sure he would never wake up.

He tried praying. Tried to pick the appropriate

saint to pray to – the Saint of Lost Causes? The Saint of Calamity? Was there such a thing as a Saint Who Kept Earthquake Victims Alive? But then his mind went blank and he couldn't remember any saints' names so he gave up and started praying to the Basketball Hall of Fame.

O Most Loving, Most Gentle Kareem. Save me.

O Most Skilful Larry Bird. Save me.

O Most Powerful Michael Jordan. Save me.

Save me, please.

And then he prayed to God and made the sort of pledges a boy thought worthy of a second chance – that he would take out the garbage for his mother every night, that he would eat the bitter melon in the stew instead of leaving it on the side of his plate, that he would do better in sciences so that he would grow up to become a rich and famous doctor and look after his parents when they were old.

And then he wept.

And when he finished weeping, there was nothing to do but pray again.

That the pain would stop.

That the darkness would lift.

That the phone battery would come back to life.

And then the cellphone lit up again and he

thought, My prayer worked! A miracle! But it did not ring or beep.

In fact, it wasn't the phone at all. He realized the light was coming from a chink in the distance. And the chink became larger and larger and then a shadow appeared.

'Henry?' a voice called. 'Henry, are you there?'

And Jabby spat some rubble from his mouth and replied in a voice that almost sounded like his own, 'Please, it's not Henry any more. It's Jabbar. Short for Kareem Abdul-Jabbar.'

16
Andi

Ve had to return the trophy.

The Colts sniffed around and it was not hard for them to find out that Rocky's Secret Weapon was in fact a girl. Their school wrote a stiff letter to Saint Sim's.

The Souls (and I) did five days of detention.

But it didn't matter.

We won the game, didn't we? The fact that I was a girl was a technicality. The team knew it. The whole of Saint Sim's knew it. The entire league knew it. The Colts never lived it down.

None of us ratted on Mrs Green: nobody ever needed to know that she took me to her office and helped me pass myself off as a boy.

It wouldn't have done to rat on our new coach.

Turns out Mrs Green was a fully qualified basketball coach. She signed on as Saint Sim's Basketball Coordinator and immediately set up a girls' team. I play point guard, of course.

Bernardo was fine.

All the time, I had thought it was the pituitary tumour. I Googled it once and read a few horror stories, people growing big heads, big hands or big feet because of a tumour in their pituitary gland. And people who grew to seven, eight, nine foot but died before they were old.

But afterwards Mum explained that the operation had not been for a tumour. It had been something else.

'It was an aneurysm, a weak blood vessel in his brain that was about to burst,' Mum said, glancing at Dad, who smiled encouragingly. 'The doctors operated just in time. He's going to be fine.'

'But what about the tumour?'

Mum was silent for a heartbeat.

'Well, they scanned him again, took more blood tests to check his hormone levels.'

'And?' Why was she being so blank? I steeled myself for some bad news.

'It's dead.'

'Dead?'

'It's a miracle. The tumour is dead. His blood tests show that it has stopped releasing the growth hormone that makes Bernardo tall. It's not doing anything any more.'

A miracle. My mouth dropped open.

'What does it mean?'

'That's it. Bernardo isn't going to grow any taller.'

'Is he going to grow any shorter?'

'Of course not. He'll just be eight foot tall for ever.'

And I was glad.

Because I like Bernardo exactly the way he is.

Epilogue
Bernardo

The bad headache didn't go away for weeks after the operation. But it was no longer the jagged knife turning and turning in my brain. And when it went, it was gone for good.

And the most inescapable fact was that I was alive.

From my hospital bed I could see out of the window to the rooftops below. There were the fields, so green, with the grey rectangle of the asphalt basketball court where I saw Andi play for the first time. Yellow brick houses swept up the brow of a hill. That roof must be Saint Sim's. Somewhere just beyond was our house. Our home.

And beyond, over oceans and continents, lay my other home.

Mama got me one of those international phone cards and I spent an hour talking to Jabby about the earthquake. He said Timbuktu was selling T-shirts that said *SURVIVOR* across the chest. He was making a killing.

'Have you got one?'

'Of course!' Jabby said. 'Even your auntie wears the T-shirt. It's practically the uniform in San Andres!'

I was afraid that the village would blame me for the earthquake but the fact that there were no fatalities was seen as something of a miracle.

According to Jabby, Old Tibo now says that my power reaches across the world and will always keep our village safe.

I don't know about that.

Some people might think so. Some people say it was a miracle that my tumour died. That it was a miracle that the people of San Andres survived one of the worst earthquakes the world has seen.

I wouldn't know.

I am just a boy with a mother and a stepfather and a sister.

That's miracle enough for me.

Acknowledgements

In memory of Ujang Warlika, the Indonesian giant who only briefly enjoyed his time as a basketball star.

My daughter Mia, who faithfully assures me I am an author when I don't feel like one; and my sons Nick and Jack, who keep faith with basketball even though they live in the wrong country.

My big little sister Joy Ramos, who told me Ujang's story.

My niece Camille Ramos, an awesome basketball player, who provided the inspiration for Andi.

To my Huckleberry friend, Mandy Navasero, from whom I've borrowed the name Amandolina.

Fe B. Zamora, flat-mate in a previous life, who one late night told me the story of a pretty girl bitten by a rabid dog.

Rachiel de Chavez, whose legal work has helped many families like Bernardo's over the years – and who tells me the system today is much improved: nurses from other countries are now allowed to bring their immediate family when they come to the United Kingdom.

The creators of *The More the Manyer* and *Without Further Adieu* for providing a field guide to barok English.

Letty Jimenez-Magsanoc and Eugenia D. Apostol – my writing heroes.

The writers who generously commented on my work in progress: Miriam Halahmy, Helen Peters, Paolo Romeo and Christine Vinall, as well as Malorie Blackman, Melvin Burgess, Kathleen Duey and Fiona Dunbar, for their support.

The kind folks at Caffé Nero in Highgate, who know that I like my Americano black with one shot, and that I like a tall glass of ice cubes with my soft drinks, whatever the season.

Fiona Dunbar for opening the door.

My Philippine publisher, Ramon Sunico, who found me on Facebook, and Frankie Joaquin Drogin, who brought us together.

Hilary Delamere, David Fickling, Bella Pearson and the denizens of DFB and Random House for making my dreams come true.

My mom, Cynthia Lopez Quimpo, who gave me a love of books, and my dad, Orlando Quimpo, who gave me patience.